Now & Again

The Ecstatic
Doggerel of
Samuel Beast

Every Now & Again Something Wonderful Happens . . .

Published by The Writers' Collective   •   Cranston, Rhode Island

Now & Again

The Ecstatic Doggerel of Samuel Beast

ISBN 1-59411-016-6

Library of Congress Cataloging-in-Publication Data

Beast, Samuel,
  Now & again : the ecstatic doggerel of Samuel Beast.
     p. cm.
  ISBN 1-59411-016-6 (alk. paper)
  I. Title: Now and again. II. Title.
  PS3602.E26N69 2003
  811'.6--dc21

                              2003011392

Printed in the United States of America

Published by The Writers' Collective • Cranston, Rhode Island

Special Thanks to

those who showed me how real friends can get you through times of no money
better than money can get you through times of no real friends

and to

The Writers' Collective
www.writerscollective.org
and
Fidlar Doubleday Inc.
www.fidlardoubleday.com
for making it possible to publish *Now & Again*
in the form visualized.

All we are saying is

Give Now A Chance!

Tree of Myths

A distant howl. Creeping over the horizon is a pack of wild Doggerel!

Section One

Preface:

What is Doggerel?

Doggeroodles

Religious Doggeroodles

Doggerel!

is a little twitch on the face of what's been taught,
a serendipitous glitch in the machinery of words and thought.

8

Preface:

What Is Doggerel?

Once upon a time, verses that did not adhere to the assigned mechanics of poetic convention were dismissed as doggerel. Thus, for centuries the term *doggerel* has languished in literary pits of disrepute. No one has cared to stake a claim on this nomenclature as their own. . . until now.

So here I am (a modest, shy, almost reclusive individual), required to expound upon the virtues and necessity of doggerel.

Ahem. . .

This is more difficult than it seems. I think I'll have to ask in advance for your forgiveness concerning my weird sense of humor. Also for occasional outbursts of intensely aesthetic/erotic imagery. I am sorry for the loss of dignity incurred by including **Doggeroodles** and **Religious Doggeroodles** in this Preface. But I do not apologize for doggerel.

Doggerel Defined

dog•ger•el **-n.** Verse of a loose, irregular rhythm.
Writing that makes up its own rules as it goes along.
[Medieval] Poor, worthless.
Example on following page:

Doggerel

Doggerel ain't got no pretensions
when it slips in and out
of the dimensions
that literature can allow.
Present, past and future tents
get blown away
in the passionate winds of Now.
Herds of metaphors
gallop singing and mixing and shrieking
through the storm,
baring their fangs and rolling their eyes,
oblivious to the academic scorn
that would confine them
to a given meter and rhyme,
that would allow them to pass
just one at a time.
Any person can be
first, second or third
as beauty precedes telling
and meaning exceeds
the sum of the words.
High doggerel is the
sensuality and delight,
tenderness and rage,
of the human spirit
breaking free
from a rusty little cage.

Like a mother tongue, Doggerel sometimes sprouts new words – offshoots of itself like **Dogguerilla** and **Doggeroodles**.

About the Author

I ride the back of sensationalism,
giving away jewels
to all who will listen.
I'm not a poet,
I'm a dogguerilla.

- Samuel Beast

An Introduction
to Doggeroodles

Doggeroodles cannot boast of any intention so lofty as *intention*. An artist might, say while talking on the phone, absentmindedly scribble a doodle on a scratch pad. Soon as his intellect's been distracted, his senses of line and composition degenerate into slackers that go wherever they feel like going. They leave a trail behind like a school of used prophylactics swimming in the wake of a yacht. Doodles and Doggeroodles are sometimes too rich to be ignored, but are difficult to incorporate into anything remotely like a serious work of art. That's why they stand here awkwardly at the beginning, sort of an egregious welcoming committee to **Now & Again**. The first in line to shake your hand is **John's Soul**.

John's Soul

One day John was picking his nose when he got hold of something that felt like it was part booger and part snot, felt as he pulled it out like he was emptying the entire space behind his eyes, felt like it would never stop. Then he felt a final throb, heard a pop and it all came out with a plop onto his desktop. At first it was a shapeless blob not any larger than a small tomato. But as he watched in disbelief. . . it grew, becoming translucent as it expanded. Very quickly it took on the size and shape of a large cat, transparent as glass. John blinked his eyes and looked again. It was now as big as a cow and had the opacity of a soap bubble. When it filled the entire room, he just sat there in the middle. It was thin as air but he could tell it was there by the way it sometimes would shimmer. "I'm inside an invisible hole," he muttered as he realized that what he'd just extracted was his soul.

He decided he could more calmly consider this phenomenon if he could escape it for a while. With a self-congratulatory secret smile he slipped out the door and slammed it behind him. But the shimmer oozed out through the crack below the door panel like the ocean pouring through the Suez Canal. It filled the hall and proceeded ahead of him as he ran down the stairs. He opened the door to the street and his soul stretched out to everywhere. It raced to the horizon. It engulfed the sky. John scratched his head and uttered a sigh which didn't immediately disappear, but came back like an echo to his ears.

He hadn't walked a block when he saw a kid in his early teens discarding onto the sidewalk an empty plastic bag from which he'd been eating jelly beans. "Hey!" said John, tapping the boy on the shoulder. "Hope you don't take this as a reprimand from someone who's older. But since we both have to live inside my soul, I'd appreciate it if you didn't litter." The youngster's eyes grew wide with fright. He turned and ran till he was out of sight. As John slowly walked away, he made a mental note to be more careful about what he might say.

He began to notice that cars and trucks were emitting fumes, that poisonous gasses were passing out of smokestacks in cloudy plumes, that there were reports on the news about chemical warfare and nuclear bombs, that children were crying and so were their moms, that people were angry and tense, that the population of his soul was extremely dense, that forests and entire species were being decimated. No one except for him appreciated that it was his soul they were all dwelling within. It was unbearable.

So he didn't linger. He exhaled till he could tell he was on the verge of death. Then he plugged his right nostril with an index finger and inhaled a breath so prolonged that it sucked his soul right back to where it belonged: out of sight and out of mind.

Humanitarian

I once met a woman who told me her special gift for humanity was to have sex with the dying.

"Really?" I asked. "Don't you find that depressing?"

"Not actually. We're all dying," she replied, unzipping my fly.

Sky

A grasshopper born blind
because of too much light ultraviolet
takes a dive of faith into the sky
and discovers he can fly.
"Wings are better than eyes!" he cries
as he flexes his knees
for another great leap.
Meanwhile
the sky is a beautiful woman
wearing blue and white lingerie
with naked thighs and raindrop eyes,
with grasshoppers gliding on her breezes
and me sliding in and out between her sighs.

Flies

I've been watching flies (just for the sake of swatting them). I have observed that flies engage in a number of reprehensible acts. These include necrophilia, cannibalism, eating each other's excrement and incessant public copulation.

It is the final item on this list that disturbs me. I was once informed about incessant public copulation (IPC) by an infallible guru. He told me IPC was a privilege exclusively reserved for the virtuous. "In the afterlife," he stated, "the truly righteous shall be rewarded with incessant public copulation." Now, as I've said, this dude was infallible. He spoke only the word of God. He told me so himself.

So I've been thinking. When people die and think they've gone to heaven, what if they've actually transmuted into being flies? But, of course, with those weird eyes they would think their antennae were halos and their wings angelic. While fornicating with recently squashed repulsive insects, they might think they're gently, erotically awakening a sleeping angel. While devouring the flesh of their brothers and sisters, perhaps they imagine they are taking little bites of tropical melon. They probably think fly shit is caviar. Since flies have no sense of time, all this seems eternal to them.

And God laughs.

Panic Addiction

I'd like to propose a new category of emotional disorder to be known as *Panic Addiction*. I think this could easily get into the *New York Times'* top ten psychiatric diagnoses along with such blockbuster hits as *Bipolar* (too happy or too sad just for the heck of it) and *Attention Deficit Disorder* (not prone to focus for long periods on subjects of little interest such as parental lectures). *Panic Addiction* (PA) is sort of the opposite of *Anxiety Attacks,* which seem to occur for no reason. PA is based on the conviction that if one does not have good cause for panic, one is misunderstanding the situation. *PA* is often associated with *Control Freak Syndrome* (*CFS,* in which one is convinced it is a matter of survival to control the outcome of events). The primary characteristic of *PA* is that if a situational crisis does not exist, the subject is compelled to create one. This could be referred to as *getting a fix* for the *Panic Addiction.*

I can picture people with advanced degrees staking out this territory as the area of their expertise. I can also imagine geographically localized variations, such as *Philadelphia PA.* All it would take to get this condition on the map is a proprietary prescription drug to sweep its symptoms under the rug.

Subtle

Light touches skin with shadow
shadow perhaps of a leaf fluttering
fluttering phantom shadow upon your skin.
Your skin responds with goosebumps.

Religious Doggeroodles

This is where Doggeroodles attempt to cross the line from the ridiculous to the sublime. They don't quite make it all the way. They balance clumsily on the tightwire between. They are terrified of falling to either side.

Lilith and Eve

Eve has an alter ego named Lilith. Each of them claims to express the feminine. Lilith is the innocent sensuous one while Eve believes her instincts are the seed of sin. Lilith is strong and brave. Eve is willing to be Adam's slave.

Lilith sometimes emerges from the wilderness to remind Adam who the original Woman always has been. Now each moment each woman may decide if it's within the paradigm of Lilith or Eve she will abide.

Eve's Complaint

When I agreed to become this man's chattel, I didn't know I'd be haunted by my own shadow. One flip of a coin, one toss of the dice, it was a matter of luck. Now she's the one who always gets to have fun and I'm stuck with having to be nice. Oh, sure. I get to be secure, to have a house and a car and kids and a yard while she dances naked in Nature and behaves like a slut. Adam glances at me in my apron and stares at her with her cute little butt.

Is this what happens when you try to be realistic while following your dream? Is she the straw that broke the camel's back in midstream? Am I cursing my candle under a bushel? Is it the old question of which came first, the chicken or the road? Is this the myth of kissing a prince who turns into a toad?

I guess, dear Lord, what I'm trying to say is that I can go on living with what I've been given if you just keep that damn Lilith always behind us and very far away.

Sensuality Precedes Language

Butterfly Lucy smiles, looks in your eyes and says, "Language can be noble and yada, yada, yada. But when all women are free of the constraints we've been taught, the couple thousand years that follow will be the Nympho Millennia. Then cunnilingus will be revealed as the mother tongue that comes before all words."

Burning Bush

When Moses realized
that every mortal creature was
conceived to die,
the burning bush appeared
before his inner eye.
For each that dies,
more are born.
Thus forever on fire and
never consumed by the flame,
the bush told Moses,
"I AM THAT I AM is my name."

*Enough of Doggeroodles,
at least for this book. All
the pages that follow are
pure doggerel.*

Section Two

Sleeping Beauty
My Gaze
Dream
Embrace
Sideshow
Beauty And Beast

If it were a literary movement, doggerel might have been known as the
Just Let Me Get The Head In, Momma school of writing.
Here is

Aphrodisia!

Explicit eroticism doesn't have to remain in the insane, inane, banal domain of sweaty, sleazy, half-blind pornographers. Nor can human sexuality be defined within the clinical fascism of sex education texts. Doggerel nudges sensuality toward its rightful place in mythology as the intimate, passionate source of Life

The temple of the natural goddess has eyes and lips and nipples.

Sleeping Beauty

Only an awakened man
can rouse the sleeping beauty
when she's passing through
this mortal form
as though she were
the mortal form
instead of this passing.
She thinks she has a name
but her real name can't be spoken.
And even though she's forgotten me,
her promise can't be broken.
For she told me in a passion of truth
that she'd awaken whenever I called,
that she would arise
like morning
from the slumber
of the mortal stranger,
that she would open her curtains
and stand there naked
trembling on the brink
of total awareness
breathing musical air
through the pores of her skin
absorbing my gaze
to the Goddess within.

My Gaze

There is nothing to think about.
Your arms are bare.
Slip out of your blue jeans
so that your legs too
can feel the air.
I want to see you
clothed only in shadow and light.
I want to explore the grace of
your moments and gestures,
the sensations of your body's textures,
to be the hero of
your erotic adventures.
And when I've kissed you
and pinched you,
stroked you and fingered you,
licked you and bit you
and felt you till
you're ready for me
as the sky is for a tree,
then I'll roar as I enter you
and together we'll ride
on the neck of a dragon
or the back of a dolphin
through living moist caverns,
through tunnels of loving,
with your warm breath on my lips,
with heat where we touch
with my hand on your belly,
with our nerve endings ablaze.
Can you feel all this
when I give you my gaze?

Dream

I dreamed of a rainforest,
the day's rays dipping
into pools of light,
nights rain dripping
into puddles
in the shadows of moonlight.
Animals were cooing and clicking
and screeching and moaning
while you and I
played naked in our wild domain.
Like the animals
we had no opinions
and we had no names.
Your skin received my touch
as the petals of a flower being brushed
by the wings of a butterfly.
Your lips received my kisses
as trees receive breezes,
as birds are received by the sky.
The nectar-moist down between your legs
was sending secret messages
to my fingers and my tongue
and soon they sweetly did reply.
We were slippery together
along the river's banks.
We were deep into the currents
in a wriggling, rhythmic dance.
We were racing through the tropics,
we were floating in the stream.
We were making love together
as we were passing through the dream.

Embrace

You look so sensitive
and I can hear the
longing
in your secret sighs:
birds that are eggshell white
with lavender shadows
flying through vast and empty skies.
I touch your face
with my finger like a tongue,
with my vision like a dragonfly,
with my words like a song.

And beneath your dress
is a tactile place,
a tactile place indeed.
I feel your touch,
you feel me feeling.
It's almost too much,
almost takes us out of time,
leading us to remove the garments
of honesty and pretense
and nakedly experience each other
doing that old skin-to-skin dance.
Yow! We're soaring on the winds
of now and it's very sweet,
makes us ready to ride, ready to fly,
ready to love until we cry,
ready to live until we die'
ready to die until we're born.
This moment of joy is ours to explore
and uncover in each other before it's gone.

Sideshow

Here I come,
stumbling, vomiting, juggling,
throwing up live flowers,
fireflies and birds.
It's an amusing show
but I leave a trail of my own blood
wherever I go.
Because I want you so.
Because when you're gone
I walk in sandals
made of thorns,
freeze at night
and melt in the morning
recalling dreams
of kissing you on the mouth
and breathing your breath
and dropping all my doubts
into the magic fire of yes.

Beauty and Beast

The moment first we met
she was sitting beneath the sky
trying not to cry.
When I stopped to ask her why
she looked me in the eye
and said
"Everything must die."

I said,
"I know how you feel.
But until they die, hummingbirds fly.
Seeds go and grow
wherever the wind blows
and even after the flowers are gone,
the movement that happened
is like a song."

"That was pretty," she said with a smile.
"Can you stay for a while?"
"I suppose that depends," I replied,
"on if I may kiss your lips
and kiss your skin
and kiss you deep inside."
"Oh!" she exclaimed.
"But you're old and you're ugly and fat!"
"I'm sorry," I answered.
"But if you can't see past that
you'll never know me for who I am.
I guess I'll just be on my way."
Then as I turned to leave,
 she whispered, "Stay!"

Interlude

And the pale morning welcomed me onto sidestreets where I caught glimpses of her beauty as she stepped out of her bath. "You're not so different from a peeping tom," she laughed, loving it, dressing and undressing for me again and again, her many forms of nakedness unfolding in the kaleidoscope of my senses, refracting like an opal in the structures of my mind.

Sweet Cosmic Mama

Section Three

Lili And Boboo

Ghost Story

Physician, Heal Thyself

Sometimes Mr. E and Miss Tickle disappear into the mists of everyday life.

Earthplane Tales

Lili and Boboo

The exhaust system on his pickup truck was held together with coat hangers and duct tape. That was one of the many temporary fixes in his life. He didn't like to read, couldn't spell, was convinced that his eternal soul was headed for Hell. Once in a while, he did what he knew was right. Like the night he didn't screw that sixteen year old girl when she turned off the light and whispered his name. Or the times he controlled his temper instead of starting a fight. All in all, he felt, he had no illusions about himself. He was a hard-drinking man who was skilled with his hands. He could fix electric or plumbing and put up a sheet of drywall or two. But he knew that no one was any better than him. And he never thought he was better than you. Some called him Robert, Rob or Bob. But his friends all knew him as Boboo.

One morning his intention to work was undermined by a hundred dollar bill he happened to find in the pocket of some old jeans he was about to wash. "Damn!" he cried as he examined it. Then he exclaimed "Damn!" again and walked out to the truck. Country music turned up loud, he drove straight to Jason's Bar and Grill.

"**Welcome to Jason's
Hours 10AM to 2AM
Mon thru Sat**" said the sign on the locked door. Boboo squinted at his watch. It was 10:05. He knocked on the glass first with his knuckles, then with his ring.

The lock clinked. The knob turned. The door opened and there stood Lili, looking pretty like a fallen angel. "Hey, Boboo," she said with a smile. "Sorry. Seems like I've been here forever. Guess I lost track of time."

As he followed her back to the bar, his entire universe narrowed down to a wiggling, twitching vision of her butt. He wondered if she'd walk the same if she didn't know he was looking. *Yeah,* he decided. *I bet she walks like that even when she's alone.*

She leaned on the bar across from him and playfully glanced into his eyes. When he returned the gaze, she looked away. Studying her hands, she asked, "So, what do you want?"

He couldn't resist, grinned and said, "How about the prettiest little chick in town?"

"Flatterer," she fluttered her lashes at him. "I bet you tell that to all the girls."

He lowered his eyes in a passable imitation of someone who's shy as he replied, "Well, no. Not *all* of 'em."

"Right." She smiled. "Well, what will you have?"

"Whiskey and beer," he muttered like someone reciting a litany, "Heavy on the whiskey and mix 'em please. You know that."

She unwrapped a frozen pack of Jason's homemade chili and dumped it into the pot, added two pitchers of water and closed the top. "Yeah, yeah," she said. "Liquid breakfast?"

"Celebration," he replied. "Just found a little cash I didn't know I had."

Three boilermakers later found Boboo in a booth nodding into a semi-lucid dream about his youth. He was on the high school track team, leaping over a hurdle when he realized this jump could just keep going up and up.

"BOBOO!!" With the shrill cry of those two syllables, his eyes blinked open. "No! God damn you!!" Lili's voice, kind of hysterical. He turned his head and what he saw sobered him in an instant.

There were two men. A skinny one who was sneering and leering as he held Lili's arms twisted behind her back. And a huge outlaw biker who had pulled her sweater up and her bra down. He was laughing raucously as he felt up a naked breast. Terror and rage performed a duet on the stage of Lili's tear-covered face.

Without a thought of what he was doing, Boboo was up and fully adrenalized. "Hey!" he shouted as he grabbed the biker's shoulder.

The biker was six-foot-four of muscle, fat, hair, dirt and tattoos. He whirled around, ready to fight. But he wasn't ready for a single punch in the face that broke his nose, knocked out two teeth and swept him into unconsciousness.

The ectomorphic stranger who'd been restraining Lili suddenly felt extremely vulnerable. Boboo looked straight into his face. The man had pockmarked cheeks. His eyebrows raised and frowned in rhythms random and manic while his eyes rolled around like a horse in a panic. He released Lili and ran for the door, elbows and knees all akimbo reminding Boboo of a clown on stilts.

Boboo ran out the door to see the fellow's long limbs stretch toward one of two Harleys parked at the curb. Glancing over his shoulder, the would-be rapist recoiled in a startle reflex at Boboo's close proximity. No time to start the bike. He ran down the street like a giraffe in flight and disappeared around a corner.

Boboo stared after him a moment, then went back inside. There was Lili, trembling and wiping her face with a napkin from the bar. He said, "I'm going to call nine one one."

"I already did," she replied. "I also called Jason and told him to get his ass down here." As though to illustrate her words, Jason came running down the steps from his apartment while the front door opened and two cops walked in.

"The fellow you knocked out calls himself *Atilla,*" one of the policemen told Boboo. "Sounds like the other man was *Sneak.*" An EMT, ambulance driver, two more police and tow truck guy came and went. Then the bar was very still.

Jason peered at Lili from the space between his thinning hair and his double chin. "Listen, kid," he said, "I know you're shook up. What they did was a sin. But you gotta stay. No way I can handle the lunch crowd and do the cooking by myself."

"Shove it!" she snapped as she headed for the back door, Boboo following.

In the lot behind the bar they rushed blindly through bright morning sunlight to her car. She was parked in the space between a dark green trash bin and the dry cleaners next door. She fumbled to open her purse with shaking hands. "You're not ready to drive," Boboo said gently.

An under-nourished young calico cat jumped out of the dumpster and started rubbing against his leg. He picked the kitty up and scratched behind her ears. She responded with a loud purr. "You're going to be okay," he told Lili.

"I know that," Lili (with a tear balancing on mascara) said. "I just need to cry a little. You know?"

"Yeah, get it out of your system," Boboo replied. He tried to put the cat down so he could give Lili a hug. But the cat clung with its claws to his shirt and skin. It purred louder.

Lili began weeping like a little girl who's been hurt. Gasping for breath between sobs, she cried, "You don't know what it's like… " Her hands were clenched together at her forehead, shoulders hunched up to her ears. "You don't know what it's like to be a woman."

"I'd be the first to admit that," Boboo answered in a voice hoarse and hushed and slightly choked.

"You don't understand!" She sobbed, liquid shadows of eye makeup streaking down her face.

"Then tell me," he said. "I really want to know."

"You…" she took a deep breath, concentrated and got a powerful grip on herself. Looking into his eyes she said in almost conversational tones, "You're surrounded by this energy of male sexual hormones. Teen agers, old men, losers, egomaniacs, wimps, cute guys. All of them. Almost all the time."

"Yeah. I can see that," Boboo responded.

"If you know how to play with their horniness, or even just manage it, it's your power," she said. "If you don't know, it's deep trouble. If you get afraid of it, you're dead." She kicked the dumpster. "Then you're a punctured love doll in the trash, still being violated. Being chewed on by rats till there's nothing left."

"Oh, shit!" he exclaimed.

"And those guys this morning really scared me. So what do I do if I'm afraid now? Lock myself in my apartment? Hide behind some guy who wants to own me? Become a man?"

"Well," he said, "do you mind if I ask a kind of dumb question?"

"You mean besides 'do I mind if you ask a dumb question?'"

"Yeah, besides that." And he thought, *Good. She still knows how to be funny.*

"Go ahead. Ask."

"What I'm not sure I get is. . . " he paused and scratched his chin, then started again. "Are you afraid of men? Or is it that you're scared of getting afraid?"

She began shaking her head. "Afraid of men? Huh uh." She frowned. Her head stopped shaking. Her eyebrows raised. She broke into a smile. "That's it, Boboo! You got it exactly! That's twice today you've saved me!" She gave him a quick kiss on the lips and said matter-of-factly, "I'm going back to the bar. I've got a shift to work."

"You better wash your face."

She opened her purse, extracted a small mirror and glanced at it. "Oh, god!" she laughed. "I look awful."

"No, you don't." Boboo's words rang with sincerity and conviction.

"Thanks. I'm on until seven or whenever that bitch, Jen, comes in. Okay?"

"Yeah," he grinned while the kitty crawled up to his shoulder and licked his ear. "Get going. Jason'll be real glad to see you."

Ghost Story

Sometimes I wonder how I can love you so much when you're totally insane. You're aware how green your eyes are when you're looking at me, aren't you? You peer from behind red hair that's fallen over your face. You're curled up on the couch. You say, "I'm terrified of not being able to pay our bills!"

"We've got plenty of money," I say. "You know that paying our bills is not even a problem."

"I mean before," you tell me. "Or maybe later. I'm not sure."

Maybe I love you because the only time you're not crazy is when we're making love. That's when you wrap yourself so intimately around my longing for you. That's when we skinny dip in the present together. No talk about the child you've never had – will never have – being with you all the time. No tears for that which did not happen. No yearning for that which did. My tongue on your skin is world enough. Your tongue on mine. Our fingertips merge. When we make love, you're totally present. And I, who have always been so rational and analytical. . . that's when you drive me out of my mind.

The doctors say there's a new medication that may cure you of your obsessions and delusions. I think we've heard that tale before. I wonder what you were like before the miscarriage that pushed you over the edge. I wish I'd known you then. Your arms around my neck and your head on my chest, you need to be comforted. I tell you I love you and you snuggle closer, getting tears and snot all over the front of my shirt.

Do you remember the time we went to the zoo? A pair of young leopards were mating. They were stretched out, nibbling so gently at each other with little yowls punctuating the rhythm of their lunges and thrusts. At one point she looked at him over her shoulder and their golden eyes locked together as they wiggled and squirmed. He kept falling out. You and I smiled at each other. The same thing had happened to us in that weird position we tried. Two overweight, middle-aged women came into the building. We weren't really aware of them till we heard one say as they walked away, "That's disgusting! They should go home and watch pornography. At least we wouldn't have to see them like that." The spell was broken. You gave me that wild-eyed, green-eyed panic look. "Let's get out of here! Quick!" you whispered. I knew there was nothing I could say to make you feel better.

All the way home, you stared out the passenger window and blinked back tears. When we walked in the door, you began talking excitedly about a puppy you wished we had. Then you closed yourself in the studio. You're a talented artist. But all you paint is pictures of tiny coffins from every possible angle, floating in streams, on the tops of mountains, levitating in clouds, being lowered into graves. You're breaking my heart! I guess we'll try that new medication. Who knows? Maybe it will help.

Physician, Heal Thyself

Photo by Sunny Cintamani

Episode 1

Of course I tell you this in the strictest confidence. That may sound foolish since you don't know my name. But I need to pour these things out before they spill everywhere. And I'm afraid to talk about it. I might inadvertently drop clues, hints like a trail of bread crumbs that lead back to my identity. Who I am has become so uncertain, you see. I have to protect this me who has so much to lose! All right. I'll trust you because I must. I'll reveal just enough so you understand.

Maybe it's the cumulative suffering of my patients. Or the overpopulation of fierce details in my work load. When I was young I thought of it as an exhausting adventure, the price I had to pay. I always had more strength in reserve. Now my emotional assets are exhausted. But I can't kid myself. What I've been experiencing is not simple burnout. It's an anomaly, psychotic episodes in an otherwise healthy mind. Schizophrenia. Another personality emerging to claim the world as its own. Dismissing the real me as though I were flotsam and jetsam of some sort of awakening. I've seen a multitude of schizophrenics in my day. And these delusions don't fit the pattern. There's no sense of grandeur to expand my ego's territory. Quite the contrary. Nor is there any flight from imagined persecution. These aberrations begin with the feeling that my normal persona is a fiction I've spent a lifetime constructing. Then the other personality emerges, seeming authentic and utterly credible. But I'm getting ahead of myself. Let's go back.

My memory of the events leading up to that first incident may be a bit colorized by hindsight. For example, I recall a vague uneasy sense of anticipation that began early the morning when Wasika was being interviewed. He was brought to staff meeting because he had somehow breached security. Beneath his customary charm and manners, I could see he was agitated.

"I respect your line of authority," he said, "and you have my truthful word not to wander again."

Kelly, who was responsible for the night shift, demanded, "How did you get out of your room?"

Wasika stared at his own hands and answered, "I have no importance. I walk like a ghost and no one sees me."

"I saw you!" Kelly snapped.

"Yes. You saw me," admitted Wasika.

Kelly was becoming more agitated. "How did you unlock your door?"

Sweat coalesced on Wasika's black skin in the air-conditioned conference room. "It just open," he replied.

Kelly pushed his glasses up to his forehead and glared at Wasika. "Bullshit! We're talking state of the art electronic lock up, damn near a hundred thousand dollars. And you expect me to believe 'it just open'?"

Wasika, the nephew of an African prince, received his education in Italy, England and France. He had a Master's degree in engineering. Kelly, on the other hand, was an orphan who had worked hard for nearly two decades to become an excellent psychiatric RN. It occurred to me that the exchange between them was as much a clash of class and culture as circumstance.

"Mr. Kelly," I intervened, "please show some respect."

Kelly stood up, his hair red and his face red. He howled, "He was in the nurse's station!"

"I know," I answered calmly and with finality. Then turning to Wasika, "How did you get out of your room?"

"Door just open."

I instructed Teitlebaum to have Wells Fargo come check their system. Let *them* tell us how he could have gotten out. I considered adding valium to Wasika's evening medication. But in recent weeks we had struck the right combination of SSRIs and mild stimulants for him. He seemed to be coming around from his depression. I approved Kelly's order suspending Wasika's privileges until further notice. It would be a while before he left his room again.

I was soon immersed in other matters and the rigorous routine of the day took over. Two or three times during the afternoon I felt as though someone were standing behind me, just outside the range of my peripheral vision. Once, when the phone rang, I had a startle reflex. Otherwise, it was pretty much a normal day until the Code Red buzzer went off.

I was on the phone and tried to ignore the commotion until I heard "Room 314" on the intercom. Wasika's room! The next thing I remember is running up a flight of stairs while knowing the matter did not require my attention.

There was a summer storm going on outside. As I entered 314, above a distant rumble of thunder, I heard someone say, "He's dead!" The flurry of activity around me became indistinct as I focused on Wasika's hand clutching an open, empty bottle of thorazine. His face was covered with vomit, his eyes wide open. He looked very surprised. Kelly was kneeling on the floor beside him, sobbing profoundly. I would have been impatient with Kelly's loss of professional demeanor, but I believe it was his outburst that triggered my own first interlude of dementia!

It was as though I took a step back from myself. The presently adrenalized Chief of Staff of a distinguished psychiatric clinic, glorified with honors coveted by his peers, awards that had been notified by telegram and presented at banquets, author of books that sell out in hard cover before going to paperback, talented therapist whose private practice ministers to the wealthy and prominent: he was clinging desperately to these self-definitions as a tidal wave of deja vu swept over me. I was serene and perceived everything with utmost clarity.

I remembered vividly the final moments of my past mortal existence, my last breath, so long ago beneath the trees while precious Ananda laid his head on my chest and wept as Kelly was doing now.

Panic and poise wrestled for control. Panic won. The entire episode probably lasted less than a second. I turned and fled to the privacy of my office.

Perhaps Gloria was right. During one of her PMS moments, she assailed me saying, "Sometimes I wonder if there's anyone at all behind that damn mask of professionalism. Have you ever noticed you have colleagues, patients, staff and acquaintances. But no friends. Not one. Single. Friend."

I tried to diffuse her thrust. "Aren't you my friend?"

"I'm not your friend, I'm your wife! No, not even that. You don't have a life of your own, so I don't have a husband. I feel like a satellite orbiting around an icon of success!"

My cheeks had stung with the truth of her anger.

Episode 2

The one place I let my feelings out is through the clarinet. Clarinet is my muse, healer, lover and whipping boy. In the seclusion of the soundproofed den, for an hour each night before I sleep, Clarinet screams in wounded ecstasy and whispers like a sly courtesan.

And the first Friday of each month, I sit in with whatever local group is performing at The Upstage on Magnolia Street. In the last five years, more than a dozen groups have invited me to tour with them. If everything crashes around me, I could become a professional musician. There's just one catch: my other personality doesn't know which end of the licorice stick to blow through. I found that out at the climax of a solo, about three weeks after the first encounter with my alter ego.

The band that night was called *Refrigerator: The Richard Finger Group*. It was a big jazz/rock ensemble with a sound reminiscent of the 70's *Blood, Sweat and Tears*. During *Summertime*, the last number of the final set, Rich slid up to me and said, "It's yours at the cue."

Clarinet took it away from me and rampaged heartbrokenly through the melody to a crescendo of one long, sweet, clear note. As that note stretched up to the rafters, I could see myself emotionally naked, egocentric, delirious on my own pain, frightened and proud. The doctor was escaping through his music. In a warm rush of nostalgic longing, he then evaporated.

The unfamiliar instrument still poised near my lips, I stood in silence before the silent crowd. One and all, they were enraptured by distraction from their own smug, tormented illusions. I read their souls and walked offstage. There was nothing to say.

In mid-step, as the musicians once again began to play, the mortified doctor poured back into these limbs and whirled around self-consciously. The applauding crowd sounded like a herd of stampeding buffalo. Tears of relief gushed to my cheeks. I had been possessed for about five seconds.

While I wiped my face with my sleeve and Rich Finger thanked the screaming audience, one of the female vocalists rushed to my side. "Please don't go away," she pleaded. "I've never heard anything like that before! Let me buy you a drink."

A few minutes later she and I were sitting at a table with Rich Finger and a couple members of the group. Rich was the only one in the band to wear stage makeup. The flesh colored grease and eye liner looked bizarre in subdued lighting. I glanced at the others. The vocalist was exquisitely hot. Harvey, the trumpet player, was overweight and pasty-faced. Greg, the drummer, was tall, skinny and bitter. Every few minutes, someone from the audience came over to congratulate me or thank me for my performance. Rich intercepted each of them and politely but unmistakably dismissed them from our gathering.

"We're cutting our first album next week," he told me. "But the label sells mainly to teens. The producer's a sleazy jerk. He wants us to do heavier rock and less jazz. Now he's making us change the name of the band."

"Hey," interjected Harvey, "it's a start. Big national label too."

"What's the new name?" I asked.

Rich grimaced. "*Dick Finger.* That's all. What do you think?"

I had to smile. "Personally, I prefer *Refrigerator.*"

The vocalist giggled. "And he wants me to call myself Marilyn Horny. Do you think I should?"

"That's your decision," I told her. "But I think it's just a cheap shot at the name recognition of Marilyn Monroe and Karen Horney."

"Marilyn's the name my parents game me," she snapped. "And who the fuck is Karen Horney? I'm sorry! I mean, I've never heard of Karen Horney. What is she? An actress? A singer?"

"A Freudian analyst," I answered. "I guess she's not as famous as I thought."

Rich touched my hand. "You made me realize what a thin line there is between showmanship and living dangerously," he said. "The solo was great music. But stopping on that note and walking away . . . that took balls."

"Oh, Rich," complained Marilyn. "You make it sound like one of those 'spontaneous' routines you contrive and make us rehearse for weeks. Couldn't you see that it was for real?"

Rich glowered at her. "What? Did I touch your bitch button?"

She raised her eyebrows and opened her eyes wide. "Oh, Testosterone Man! You're so macho!"

Rich said, "This ain't gonna last."

Harvey mumbled, "Oh, no! They're at it again."

Greg rose from his chair to tower above them. "Cut it out, you two. We can't afford your fights. Save it till after the album's wrapped up."

Marilyn turned to me. "Are you driving?"

I nodded.

"Would you take me home? Please?"

As I said, "All right" she got up and walked toward the door. A few steps away, she turned and looked at me expectantly. I returned Clarinet to its case and stood to follow. Harvey groaned, "Oh, no!"

I glanced at Rich. "Go on," he said. "She's waiting."

Arriving at my car, she murmured, "Wow!! A Mercedes roadster convertible! What do you do?"

"I'm a doctor," I replied.

"I should have known." She laughed with a little trace of sarcasm.

"Why do you say that?"

"Because you come across so indifferent and unapproachable. You know, professional."

As we got into the car, I noticed that her pale face in profile was very near perfection.

"Well, if I shouldn't call myself Marilyn Horny, what do you suggest? I need a name." She was still looking straight ahead.

"What's wrong with your real name?"

"Marilyn Lilith? That's what kids used to call me in grade school when I was chewing bubble gum and playing with dolls. I'm a grown up now. A singer. I want a name that people will remember. Like Madonna."

"I believe that's already being used."

She gave me a tiny smile. "Yeah. Well help me out here, doctor. For some reason, I trust you."

"Must be my bedside manner," I replied quietly.

"Then come to my bedside." She turned her face suddenly away as though startled by her own boldness.

"That's a very difficult invitation to refuse," I said. "But you should know... I'm married."

"Happily?" her face still averted.

"More or less comfortably. And I have a fourteen year old daughter I love more than anything in the world."

Except for the directions she gave me through dark streets, we didn't speak again till we arrived at her address.

"Music is my calling," she said. "You know how important it is to make the right career moves."

"Yes, I do."

"Well, advise me. I need a name!"

I reflected for a moment. "Have you ever heard of Carl Jung?"

"I think so. I'm not sure."

"He was a strange fellow, tried to mix ancient superstitions with the science of psychoanalysis."

"Uh huh."

"He wrote a book about archetypes. It's full of exotic, beautiful-sounding names. I'll buy you a copy on one condition."

She raised one eyebrow. "Does the condition involve a less impersonal relationship?"

"Not at all," I said. "I want you to read the book only for the names. The rest of it is a bunch of mumbo-jumbo."

"Oh," she giggled. "At last an answer to the question, 'who are the brain police?'" Her attitude suddenly turned solemn. "I can't accept your condition. I'll get the book myself if you have to tell me what to think."

"I can respect that," I replied. "But please understand that I don't endorse his theories. I adhere strictly to the science of Freud, Skinner and Merck, Sharp and Dome. Condition withdrawn with my sincere apologies."

"I really like you!" she effervesced. "So when will you bring me the book?"

"Why don't I mail it to you?"

She pouted.

Finally I told her, "I don't have much time."

She assumed a look of grave concern. "That's really sad," she said. "Then what's the point of all your work? Just to work some more? Or do you spend most of your free time with your daughter?"

"Actually, I hardly ever see her," I confessed.

"Then bring me the book," she coaxed.

"Okay," I finally said. "Not tomorrow, but Sunday. I'll just put off the chapter I'm working on. I'm ahead of schedule anyhow."

"What time?" she asked.

"Around three o'clock."

She broke into a charming smile. "I can hardly wait!" she called as she scooted out of the car and toward the door to her building. She swung around and called back, "I'm apartment 3D." She blew me a kiss before disappearing inside.

Episode 3

I expected her to try to seduce me. But I intended to look at that roller coaster, not ride on it. I brought her the book. It was an oversized volume, beautifully bound and overflowing with color illustrations of mythological beings.

As we flipped through the pages together, Marilyn's enthusiasm was entertaining. We were examining Botticelli's *Venus* when she impulsively kissed my cheek. I looked at her coolly and she delicately kissed my lips. It was an affectionate kiss at first. Then her tongue became brazen, slipped across my upper lip and past my teeth. Her hand touched my cheek. I remained passive, secretly thrilled within the walls of my resistance. If I gave her no encouragement, she would eventually stop. That was the theory. She was still kissing me when I noticed I had begun brushing the nape of her neck lightly with one finger. Surely a neutral spot. But the skin there responded with more sensitivity than Gloria's clit.

Gloria! Little Melissa! This had suddenly gone too far! I stood up abruptly. She got up with me and tenderly wrapped her arms around me. I released myself firmly from her embrace and took a step backward. I meant to give her a look of mild reproach. Instead, our eyes began exploring each other's faces, reading subtle, exquisite, spontaneous cues. She was echoing off something within me that hadn't existed until she responded to it. *This is foreplay,* I thought. *Just looking at her face is foreplay.* I tried to say "I can't", but I couldn't. She smiled and a single photon of rejection-fear flitted across her cheekbones.

It was time to leave. But it seemed impossible to take another breath without kissing her. She saw that. She lowered her eyes in beautiful dreamlike relief and submission. *I'll kiss her goodbye and go,* I thought. But the kiss only served to dissolve us further into each other's touch.

By the time I realized that my reluctance was feeding the dynamic, we had already invented lovemaking. We had shed our clothes and our names. Both of my troublesome identities were gone. I was primal male. She was primal female. We had been engaging like this forever. We could do no wrong. Every touch or movement was choreographed by DNA. We shifted positions gracefully and often like an acrobatic ballet danced to music of gasps, whimpers and cries of joy.

48

Once I came too close to orgasm. I forced myself to remember Gloria's insistence on the missionary position, her refusal to give or receive oral stimulation, her tepid groans to express satisfaction. I started to go soft, but only for an instant. Then I was purified in a flash of sensual inspiration. I plunged like a locomotive through moist tunnels. I sipped like a cat at tender orifices. I discovered the tactile nature of my tongue on any spot of her skin. Hours flew past like seconds, but seconds lasted almost like still frames. It was getting dark outside when our bodies raced past the point of no return. I fell into a delirium of exhaustion.

I don't think I slept more than a half hour. When I woke up she was waiting for me eagerly.

"Guess what!" she enthused. "I've got a name!"

The timeless horizon crept slowly back into linear continuity. Of course, of course. I didn't come here to fall in love. "You have a name?" I asked, still somewhat dazed.

She nodded.

"Tell me," I said.

She shrugged her pretty shoulders as though to say, "what else?" "Maya," she whispered.

I looked at her blankly.

She looked concerned. "Don't you like it?"

"I don't recall who Maya was," I said.

The book was open on her naked lap. "Maya is the illusion of the world," she said. "It's Hindu. Like whatever we experience with our senses or minds is sort of a dream that happens inside us. That's all we can ever know. It's real, but it's not what it seems. It's just the seeming."

I was incredulous. "Jung said that?"

"No, not exactly. That's my interpretation. But the way I see it is what counts, because I'm Maya and Jung is just Jung."

"Jung benefits greatly from your translation," I said.

"It's not just a stage name," she said, "and it's not just a name. As soon as I read it, I said This is me!"

"Sort of a spontaneous transformation?" I asked.

"Kind of. You know, guys tell me I'm hot. Some of my friends say I'm a bitch. I can see why they'd say that. But I never felt like it was really me. I think Maya is who I've been all along. I just didn't know. So, yeah. It is a. . . what did you call it?. . . spontaneous transformation."

"I can't shift identities like that," I said emphatically.

"Why not?" she asked with a playful grin.

"I have too much to lose. I have responsibilities, people who count on me to be me. In my profession, I'd become a laughingstock."

As I spoke, an eerie feeling oozed up my spine. *Oh, God! Not now!* I thought. *Please not now!* My anxiety and dread ran in smaller and smaller circles, receding into a vacuum along with the adulterous doctor himself. I folded my legs into the full lotus position.

Maya sensed immediately that something had occurred. Her hand slipped away from me and she stood up, the book sliding onto the bed. She gave me a puzzled look.

"Hello," I said. "Beautiful, cruel Maya. I see you're still up to the same old games."

She made an incomplete gesture with her hand, as though she were going to cover her nakedness then reconsidered. "What?" was all she could say.

"You're wasting your time with him," I continued. "He'll soon be going to the other side."

"Who?"

"The good doctor. Don't pretend you don't recognize me."

"I thought you said you couldn't do this," she protested.

"He said he couldn't do this." I smiled. "He tries so hard to deny me. Whoops, he's coming back."

Clarity dissolved into confusion, calm into chaos. I was strangling on the impossibility of the situation. It had lasted more than a minute this time. And what did he mean "the other side"? I somehow mouthed, "I have to go!" in such a quiet undertone that I couldn't hear it myself.

"What happened?" cried Maya, so naked and alluring.

"I don't know," I answered, pulling on my clothes.

"Don't go!" she pleaded.

I heard myself whine "I have to" as I ran out the door.

Flight

The ride home from Maya's began with panic and progressed into pure animal terror. I had been driving in a frenzy for several minutes before I realized that I was lost. Confusion navigated me through a maze of dark, narrow ghetto streets. I was in the midst of what looked like a war zone with boarded up, burned out buildings, curbs strewn with abandoned wreckage of cars. Stop signs intruded at every corner. I probed into the darkness, searching for the small comfort of signs with street names. There were none. Anonymity sucking the last juice out of terminal poverty. Locked into first and second gears by constant stops, I felt like I was crawling on my belly through third world America. Lots of torque, but not enough velocity to escape. *This is what it will be like,* I thought, *if I don't get a grip on my mind.*

Then I came to the projects. Street lamps garishly illuminated patches of sidewalk but blackness prevailed. *"I'll cut your heart out, motherfucker..."* screamed a boom box. A frightened missionary lost alone in an African jungle night. War drums behind. War drums ahead. The Mercedes became a fatuous display of privilege and wealth. My face and hands became conspicuously white. Every streetcorner group of black males turned their incredulous or angry or arrogant or suffering faces to me. Crackheads and junkies and carjackers prowled through the shadows of my fear.

At the same time, I was attempting to calculate the rate of escalation with which delusions were encroaching upon my life. It was exponential. The first episode had lasted a fraction of a second. The next was perhaps five seconds. The one with Maya had gone on for at least a minute. There had been forty three normal years before the first attack. Three weeks till it happened again. Then, less than two days. I could have another episode at any moment and it might endure for hours.

My other self, who thinks he's Buddha, who can't play clarinet, won't know how to drive. *If he emerged right now*, I thought, *we'd simply crash.* And the attacks seem to be induced by moments of emotional intensity!

Beneath the grating mental noise of these horrors jostling into one another was the steady drone of sorrow for my compromised family. And the agonizing throb of longing for more of Maya's face and body, her touch.

By the time I arrived home, my shirt was soaked by perspiration. I was trembling with anxiety. I took a long hot shower followed by a cup of warm milk and honey. Though physically cleansed, I now possessed a tainted secret that defiled my marriage. My mind was perched on the edge of a precipice of unbearable tension. I had to make plans quickly.

I could imagine "Buddha" emerging at tomorrow morning's staff session or at the afternoon Director's meeting. I pictured myself as an inmate instead of Chief of Staff, cautiously following the rules and hobnobbing with Ron who sometimes thinks he's Jesus. Disaster around the corner! Vultures of oblivion circling my head!

If there were more time I could resign from all positions of responsibility, give notice and assist the directors in interviewing candidates for my replacement. Not possible now!

I wandered upstairs and peeked into Melissa's room. Light from the hallway gently illumined her sleeping face. She was almost a young woman now, but still slept with her arms wrapped around Big Pink Bunny. "Daddy's going away," I whispered, "I'll try to come back someday. I love you."

I went to our bedroom and turned on the soft light of the reading lamp. In deep repose, Gloria looked innocent and vulnerable. Whatever her sexual short-comings, she had always been fiercely loyal to me. She'd given her entire life over to being my mate. She stirred beneath my gaze and opened her eyes.

"Oh, you're home," she said, still half asleep. "Tomorrow will you look at my checkbook with me? Something's missing." I kissed her cheek and she slipped back into slumber.

Quickly and silently I packed an overnight bag, then hurried downstairs to the den. The letter to my secretary composed itself.

Dear Grace,

You know it's been eight years since I took vacation or a sick day. Now I must withdraw some of that accrued time. Please inform staff members and the board that my research into abnormal mental states has at last yielded results. These new findings are of such significance that I must immediately pursue them. I'll be traveling extensively, but will call when I'm able. Please cancel all appointments. Refer my private patients to Hildebrandt and send him their notes and records.
Gratefully, etc.

Unprofessional, I observed, re-reading it. *Even irresponsible. But desperate times call for desperate measures.* I left a note for Gloria saying I'd call in a few days, asking her to deliver Grace's letter and to hug Melissa for me. Then I drove to the Hilton where I paid cash and checked in under an assumed name.

The suite was a comfortable, even luxurious, retreat. I felt safe for the moment, exhausted but relieved. *Let my other personality come out and play now,* I thought. *If no one knows who I am, he can't embarrass me.* Thus, in the sanctuary of obscurity, did I calmly devise a plan to defeat the phantom of my brain.

My other self's foothold was his ability to trivialize me, to cast my normal mind in doubt. Ultimately, reality was on my side. I had a history going back to infancy, credentials, money, position, as well as knowledge gained by study and experience. My alter ego, on the other hand, was a flight of fancy, a mental aberration without factual basis. Since he existed only as a quirk of my imagination, he could have no more knowledge of the historical Buddha than myself. Which is to say none. This, I realized, was his Achilles heel! If I could undermine his conviction of authenticity, I'd be free of him.

Morning light was seeping in around the venetian blinds. I was lying on my back on the couch, still fully clothed, reflecting on my overall situation. Gradually, sleep and dreaming took possession of my thoughts. Allow me to recount the particulars:

Before these psychotic episodes began, my sense of time was different. Days flew by so quickly there was barely time to cross items off to-do lists or add appointments to my calendar. Conversations slowed me down to an impatient pause. Random details soared past like flocks of birds or an occasional singular butterfly.

Now that it could all be snatched away, I find myself proceeding so much more deliberately. Each moment is embroidered with colorful particulars and embellished by heartfelt metaphors. Conversations have become the passing lane through which I speed and swerve, ever apprehensively glancing in the rear view mirror; knowing that any moment red and blue flashing lights might materialize; that I may be forced to pull over onto a shoulder of the road; that Officer Buddha will demand to see driving credentials I've somehow lost; that he will take me away! I don't want to go, but it's impossible to resist. He takes me away!

I slept the whole day. Just woke up an hour ago, showered and made my way down here to the lounge for a drink. When you struck up conversation, I could see you were well-educated. A man of integrity. A good person. So, please tell me. What do you think?

Section Four

Doggerel has a fling with that high maintenance bitch who calls herself *Time*. The inexact artifacts of such adventures are known as

Tales of Now

CAUTION!

Tales of Now is given just for those who are ready for linear time to lose its grip. These stories, myths and allegories are filled with self kept secrets. If a tale here bores, bewilders or angers you, please skip this section entirely and enjoy the rest of the book. In a few months or years it may be worth another look.

Sweet

Cosmic

Mama

Sweet Cosmic Mama

Oh damn but I miss ya, sweet cosmic mama. You've been gone so long that my heart feels like month old cat shit in the desert, like a fossil, like a cornflake, like an empty tomb.

Then she said, "Open like a baby's eyes, now open like the sky."

And there she was: baptized by immersion into the human condition, wounded by confusions pathetically calling her name (they are crying out her name like a great flock of birds descending from the clouds to settle in a single tree), so that she quickly dresses in the flesh of all the scenery that is passing and passes away.

Oh damn but I miss ya, sweet cosmic mama. When you're not around I barely get by. I'm like a three-legged mantis trying to pray: ain't got no grace, just fall on my face. I'm in the wrong place when you're not here.

Then she said it again, "Be open like a baby's eyes; open like the sky." And she returned in a dream, moving like a mirror moves: images playing in her stillness. And moving like a moment moves: reflections in a passing stream.

We are sitting on her sofa looking at old photos together, neither of us saying a word. Our legs brush lightly ... it's ripples of fire. I pass her a sunset, murmuring, "Here, look," while our fingers touch in an exchange that lingers like a kiss. We pretend nothing is happening and avoid each other's eyes. Outside a dog yips. Bells clang and the drawbridge lifts. Years pass through without so much as a toot on a flute, that swiftly and they're gone. "This is getting too intense," she said. "I could love you this much or hate you this much, but not both at once. I can't stand it. It's all I can feel. I'm losing my mind!"

Seeking to alleviate her distress, I disguised myself in the dress of a clown in the circus where she performed. I was rich, I was witty. I was poor, I was dumb. She offered me her pity, then dismissed me with her scorn.

And the pale morning welcomed me onto sidestreets where I caught glimpses of her beauty as she stepped out of her bath. "You're not so different from a peeping tom," she laughed, loving it, dressing and undressing for me again and again, her many forms of nakedness unfolding in the kaleidoscope of my senses, refracting like an opal in the structures of my mind.

But on the other hand she wore a ring and she came awake like some fairy tale princess, finding she possessed the wisdom gem and learning how to use it, feeling Venus flowering in silent crypts of consciousness where no one could abuse it.

Meanwhile the swollen creek rushed over its banks, parting a way through thorny vines, sweeping dead branches into blissful dances that followed the current into deepening crystal pools.

A blind man plays flute in the morning. The sun is rising. Sparrows are chirping and hopping in and out of puddles that reflect the world upside-down. We are in bed together with plants growing in the windows and a soft breeze whispering all over our bodies like quicksilver, liquid abalone, mother of pearl. We are diving in and out of each other like the sparrows and puddles, just lying there side by side.

But another time I peeked under her locked door and there saw the boots of another man.

"Hey!" I cried, "Open up!" but was answered only by a passionate moan.

I fled alone into a dangerous alley where clutching hands reached out of the darkness as metal cans rattled and a sudden hot rain blew in.

There in the midst of a gust of wind, as lightning flashed and an alley cat ran past, I saw her cowering, whimpering, naked and scared.

"Wait!" I cried as she ran through a large iron gate and disappeared.

I hunted for her in the heart of the storm. Time and again she appeared to me through images that would remain after she had gone; like the still warm body of a lifeless thing, like damp foot tracks that evaporated where she had been.

At last I knew (or thought I felt) that appearances are like a magic spell, that enchantment is the meandering of mind in the grip of illusion. Armed with this bludgeon of conclusion, I set out to end my own confusion and terror. I headed at once for the Wall of Mirror, the famous fortress that surrounds the whole known world.

I passed satisfied people who were chewing on fruit, went by frightened folks who felt they had something to lose, intelligent people quoting from books, belligerent people, rebels and crooks. I passed them all by. When they called me a dreamer, I smiled at the name. And it wasn't long before I came to the Wall of Mirror.

At first all I could see was myself... though I finally noticed that I appeared within a scene: there was a path that led to a tree, a lot of sky, a little grass, and her and me.

"Mirror! Mara! Illusion!" I cried, and hurled my hammer against that great wall. I suppose I thought it would fall. Instead it cracked into hundreds of millions of pieces, each one reflecting within itself entire the sun as it rose like holy fire in the sky. Now there were countless skies and trees and hers and mes and I cried out, "What have I done!?!"

She soothed me. She touched me. She whispered in my ear.

"Someday you may wish to confess," she said, "but not now and not here."

Oh damn but I missed ya, sweet cosmic mama. Whenever you're gone, it screws up my song. All my things become thorns, my mendings get torn, and I should have never been born if you're not here. This time you've just got to say something to me about why you never stay."

She handed me ice in a silver cup as she said, "You don't satisfy my needs."

It was just a blast followed by reverberations of shock. I was as a bird convulsing in mid-flight, plummeting through the center of expanding concentric echoes of meaning.

"You're bold enough to look me in the eye," she sighed, "but too weak not to turn away. You're like a rich man pursuing the pleasures this world may offer or like a hermit attempting to avoid the sorrows of your fate. You are distracted, inattentive, with your eyes full of daydreams. You leave me too early and come to me too late."

From my limited understanding I replied, "But sweet cosmic mama, what you're saying does not make sense to me. Here we are for a moment without disguise or pretense, and you say I'm as wrong to resist as to be caught up in your hypnotic dance."

She shrugged her shoulders, smiled and replied, "Turn away while I undress and watch me in the Wall of Broken Mirrors."

As I regarded her with insolent hesitation, she cried out, "Don't you see? Everything that's happened is in perfect preparation for now. You must do what you must do!"

Shedding all my shame, discarding all my pride and stealing one last glance as I turned aside, I submitted to what must inevitably be. Chorus frogs, crickets, birds, and the wind in the trees all harmonized into a single tone: the mantra uttered by the celestial horn, which opened up into the ecstatic song of a multitude of angels being born... and suddenly faded and was suddenly gone.

Looking at last into the Wall of Mirrors with the fleeting scene reflected differently from fragment to shard, I watch in fascination the magical progression as you begin undressing, your essence to unveil. I am immersed in the warm tingling sensations of profound transformation as illusion expresses its relation to what's real about you and me. As focus emerges from distraction, I discover that what is is a passing reflection of everything that could possibly be.

There you are, inside of one small jagged-edged section: sitting naked on the end of our bed with sunlight and your hands playing in your hair and about your head. Close-up of your face as you lower your eyes and smile my way, while my still-warm sperm slides slowly and wetly down your trembling thigh. Oh my! I don't know if I can take it. Unclothing yourself you've opened me up so that my insides are unearthed like sore and aching archeological ruins exposed for the first time in millennia to harsh air and the light of the sun. With one breath I want you to stop and with the next I cry, "Keep on! Keep on!"

This is all at once knowing, really seeing, how impermanent everything is. It's the commonplace moment made rare by its loss. It's perceiving that each movement, nuance and gesture is fleeting, precious and unique as flowers that die the instant they bloom; or music that fades as I enter the room, tantalizing and unforgettable, yet I can't quite recall the tune; it's butterflies with wings melting wherever I touch; it's going by too quickly and meaning far too much.

For one bittersweet moment I cling to her image. She says "Ohhhh," and impulsively reaches out with both hands to touch my face. Then it's over and done. She's gone. I'm alone with the Wall of Broken Mirrors.

"When illusion has passed, does the sense of loss and gain remain?" I chide myself, thus momentarily evading gray specters of pain and despair. And, "Reflections seen in dew drops as they evaporate in the sunlight are soon lost like dreams or rainbows into the void from which they came. Time is death, swallowing up this moment. Death is time, dropping each verb and noun into the gaping abyss of nothingness just as though it never had been."

So did I soliloquize while treading the slender naked edge where beauty and terror are realized as the flotsam and jetsam of time's terrible tide. At last I knew that I was truly alone, that there was nothing I could ever own... for more than a moment. I deeply sighed and surrendered, felt myself submerging into the ocean of my own being, sensation and vision converging to the point where I just couldn't care. I found her there.

"You're finally catching on," she said. "At times you were such a slow learner, just as stubborn as a child."

"It no longer matters what you say," I straight-faced did reply. "Receiving is giving and dying is living and I no longer wonder why."

She was so close that I could see the pores of her skin. Our eyes were almost touching. The movement of her lips as she spoke beckoned like some long-forgotten sin.

She said, "Well now that you know that coming and going are really the same, isn't it time to abandon your sense of loss and see each moment how creation begins?"

"If you want to tempt me," I answered (for I saw through her schemes), "you'll have to understand that I'm no longer entertained by the play of circumstances or the mere poetics of how things seem. In every attempt to test if the fire was real, I've wound up being burned by the heat of the dream."

She backed away, saying, "You live as though you had something to lose or something to gain. Every time you sneak a glance in the rear view mirror, all you can see is that things disappear. You want to keep the joy and lose the pain. Whenever you discover you have a choice, all you do is whine and complain."

"Oh Woman," I cried, "I don't know who you are! Is it your wish to deceive me, or receive me, or relieve me, or bereave me? Do you know what you're doing? Do you know who I am?"

"I'll deceive you," she replied, "by being whoever your mood makes me, receive you however you take me. I'll relieve you, leave you, bereave you till dawn. And if you don't really want me, then I'll be gone."

62

"At this point," I answered, "I am beyond all desires. I have helplessly watched as each precious living moment that transpires becomes a corpse that is consumed by ongoing movement as though being scourged by the flames on a funeral pyre. And when the last white ashes are blown away by the wind, the mourning itself passes into echoes of echoes of echoes within."

She sighed, "You're so dense. You're missing everything that's subtle. I offer you a gift and you give me a rebuttal. Now open like a baby's eyes, open like the sky."

A tremor of curiosity passed through me like a convulsion in reverse, opening my heart to the meaning of her words.

She went on, "Your attitude and stance are the music to the dance you find yourself in. Like the soundtrack to a film, like a Wish Fulfilling Gem, the mood you've created sets up precisely the events that will be activated."

"Wait!" I cried out in frustration, though I couldn't help a bitter smile. "I don't mean to complain, but I have just seen every solid empirically known object slip away down Time's inevitable drain as though being sucked into an inverted cornucopia or a black hole. It's insane! I'm under so much stress! The only way things could possibly be worse is if by some unimaginable curse, I were responsible for the whole sweet mess. Please tell me I'm wrong, that you don't really expect me to believe that as I project, so shall I receive."

She laughed as though I'd said the funniest thing yet and answered, "Yes, what you give is what you get."

"There must be some way out!" I cried. "This is too much to bare!"

"I thought you could take it," she said. "I thought you no longer cared. Didn't you once look me in the eye and say that you preferred the most terrible truth to the most beautiful lie?"

"But this is like being forever alone," I moaned. "And I, who've loved mystery and the unknown, now find that anyplace I could possibly travel or reside is made up of no more than wishes and stone! And you, my darling, my heart's desire, are only an image in a broken mirror."

"Yes," she sighed, "I don't think you can get much clearer than that. But don't forget to show some respect. Because what I receive is what I'll reflect. Let me see just a little doubt and I'll throw you out on your ear and curse you and hate you and make love to your peers."

"If this is true, my life's no more than desolation, masturbation, an elaborate scam!"

She had become very cool, almost cold. "Don't be such a crybaby," she scolded. "As long as you relate with understanding instead of reacting like a fool, you'll be in perfect control."

"Of my own illusions!" I wept. "Is this all that can be?"

"It's a miracle," she replied. "If you don't get drawn into believing the tales you've conceived, eventually you'll be relieved. You'll finally see that you're both the dreamer and the dream."

"Then I have no choice but to choose, even if I don't know that I'm choosing? Even if I fall back into the illusion of winning and losing?"

"You can choose to forget what you've seen and I'll disappear. Then you'll go on searching for me in the faces and grace of women with whom you've never been ..."

"Or I can accept all this and live as someone married to the wind."

"That's it," she smiled. "Would you like to flip a coin?"

"No," I replied. "The whole coin's mine, both sides, and I'll carry it with me wherever I go. If either side becomes too much of a bother, I'll turn it over and look at the other."

"Your indecision is a bore," she said, giggling, and faded into the landscape of mountains and streams.

"Sweet cosmic mama, I see you!" I called as I walked off into the emerging horrors and delights of the earth plane and dreams.

The Birth of Now

Chapter 1

Ah, precious young one,
full of desire,
if it weren't so late
I'd reach into this fire
and pull out a tale so tragicomic
that gods would laugh
and weep with tears atomic,
such a tale that
it would eliminate
the used-up story lines
of greed and lust and hate
of soap opera palaces
and material jails,
of wars and talk shows
and scandals and sales.
Instead, my darling,
if you were inclined,
we could cut away the cultural chains
that are entwined
with the feelings and thoughts
of our hearts and our minds.
Oh, never mind the hour!
Let's just plunge into the primal power.
Let me lead you into the invisible realms
where human awareness dwells,
nakedly crying and silent in the thrill
of being one with nature's will.

Chapter 2

The cloudy skies are like a temple
of marble and light,
like holographic convergences
of vision and sight.
Here water and wind shape the land.
Here it is feeling that moves your hand.
Here consonants defer to the vowel's command
and nouns are dancers in verbs' sweet band.
Here we meet Ever who is always true,
whose words give shape
to the physics of sound,
whose sight is the constant of light,
whose touch defines
the invisible lines on the face
of gravity, momentum,
inertia and space.
Ever is the seer and Ever is the scene
and Ever has always traveled with you
no matter where you've been.
And Ever is maleness of the highest intent,
looking for the woman on whom
his passion shall be spent.
And the nymph of his destiny
with whom he will mate
is the muse of dance
and her name it is Changing.
Changing always knows
that she is naked beneath her clothes
and she sometimes flies
into the inner flows
that harmonize with the moon.
Changing is immersed in the song
of most intimate voices,
carrying the spent seed

when it falls to the earth
and nurturing the fertile egg
from start to birth.
And Changing is a dancer
like the wind in the trees
and Changing is a swimmer
like the tides in the seas.
When Ever meets Changing,
it's love at first sight.
Their first mutual glance
is a never-ender
giving birth to a being
of indeterminate gender,
a being that springs full grown
out of Changing's womb,
don't ask me how.
But I do know its name is
Now,
Now Ever-Changing.
Rising unbidden
out of oceans of potentialities,
to reveal truths hidden
within the confusion
of self-made realities,
some know him as Karma.
Some see her as Love.
Some just close their eyes
and fall when they move.
Sometimes Now will shed its skin
and leave it in a place
that people call When.
Now's song surpasses
what humans can hear,
is sung by each instant
that ever whispers in eternity's ear.
And Now dresses in any costume it can find,
the mystic robes of the enchanter

or the naked flesh of your own behind.

Now could be the brutal sound
of metal dragging across the ground
or the subtle stillness in an angel's sigh,
or just the movement of your eye.
Now dominates you totally,
Now surrenders to your whim.
Now is the perfect lover,
the fleeting her, the constant hymn.
Now is a question, an answer or a song,
or the man or woman you love
writhing on your lips and your tongue.

Chapter 3

Introducing Now to the crowd,
Samuel Beast paces the stage
and finally dares to say out loud,

> "The microphone I use to amplify my voice
>
> is actually none other than our moment of choice:
>
> NOW!!!"

Now, the microphone, bursts out of his hand
and out of shape
and becomes first a fountain
then a tornado,
then a quicksilver lake
in a mountain of pearl
with riderless horses
splashing through the shadows
and intentional divers
slipping quickly into the deep.
A light rain falls
with each raindrop a viewpoint,

a lifetime,
a breath.
And Now licks your eyelid.
He's a lover already inside you,
gently embracing
your shoulders and your breasts.
And Now whispers *"now"* in your ear
as she wraps herself
moistly around you
and rests her cheek upon your chest.

And
Now says,

> *"Hello audience*
> *witness*
> *experiencer.*
> *I am so grateful for your attention*
> *that I would give you everything in return.*
> *But the multitude turns*
> *away from me;*
> *wherever they turn*
> *I am there in disguise*
> *and though*
> *they can't see me with their thoughts,*
> *they can't miss me with their eyes.*
> *People who are caught*
> *in their own thought,*
> *who stare at the ceiling*
> *of their own hidden feelings,*
> *these people who fear*
> *what next will appear,*

who think, plan and scheme
to make life resemble their dreams,
who by confusing desire with need
become victims of their own greed,
these are some of the people
that turn away from me.
If you want to see me
you must open your eyes.
If you want to be with me
then never touch me
without feeling me.
Never tell me any lies."

Now's face dries out,
skin falls away revealing bone
which pulverizes at once to sand
and blows away. . .
except for a few grains
that collect like dew in the down
on the back of your hand.
Someone in the audience cries out
"Where's Now gone?"
and those words are incorporated into the song
along with the sound of a fly
buzzing in sunlight over a kitchen table
or a warm whispering gasp of breath in the night
or an animal's cry abandoned in flight
that echoes through twilight shadows
and from countless rocky cliffs
of how's and why's and when's and if's.
And a sob of my own slips out of my grasp
as we emerge from the trance
of believing in a future and a past

and enter into
the swirling, sweltering madcap dances
of the present moment's unknown chances.

And Now says,

"I am a dangerous lover.
You can only live with me
when you're living by the skin of your teeth,
when you're living like a cat
holding nothing back,
when you want to rise out of the masses
to kick the asses of philosophers
who walk along the shores of an ocean of vision,
blindly seeking for proof of their own opinions.
Yes, when you eat your experience
as it arrives and raw
rather than cooking the life out of it
and passing it from hand to foot to claw,
then I can be yours and you can be mine,
slipping together in and out of time,
dishonoring dogma and laughing at its clowns,
sniffing the air like a pair of hounds,
hugging the earth like stones in a field
or stylishly passing through cities and towns.
I'll lick your wounds and make them healed.
You'll fly with my wings and sing the song
of innocent lips at last unsealed."

Interlude

"If you subtract all the particulars that make a moment real," he was enunciating each word distinctly, "you can break up the imaginary empty nothing that's left into constant intervals. Make timepieces to keep everyone in step. Do you call *that* reality?"

Adrienne, ***The Last Dragon***

The Woman Who Rejected Now

For a while
Now was infatuated
with a mortal woman.
She possessed such uncommon beauty
that one would have to gasp at the grace
with which she averted her face
whenever Now appeared.
In any case, Now offered to love her
with the ten thousand slow
and quick licking tongues of Lesbos
and the divining rod of a divine god
penetrating to the heart.
In return she offered her rejection,
saying Now's movements
were much too quick,
further saying she felt more attraction
to security than to risk.
One day Now came to her as
warm water caressing her skin
in a bubble bath.
"You offer a lifetime of adventure,"
she said,
"when all I want is
the happily-ever-aftermath."

Soon she met a strange chimera,
who had just returned
from vacation on the Riviera.
By fate and his family
he had been dealt
an inheritance of
monumental wealth
and extraordinary animal features.
He was one of those mythological creatures

with the heart of a dog, the head of a man,
a baboon's body and the voice of a lamb.
His breath and his farts
constantly steamed
as he told her what she wanted to hear
about how things seemed.
He recited terrible poetry,
bleating and blahing in human words
while out of his butt
dropped steaming baboon turds.
He also had transparent wings,
appendages like those of a great bird,
though not powerful
enough for flight.
When he became excited
they fluttered and whirred,
thus fulfilling nature's intent
as they dispersed the worst
remnants of gaseous
simian excremental scent.

Because she knew
he would always be
faithful and true
and keep her safe
from anything new,
she took him as her lover
and allowed him to be
her Guardian.

This Guardian created for her
a Chamber of Security,
a windowless home
to protect all her purity
from the risky unknown.
When through a heart-shaped door
she entered the Chamber,

it was spacious and gracious
and free from all danger.
The walls were crimson and pink
in velvet and satin
with gold leaf and opals
intricately patterned.
She decorated the space
with consummate good taste
and lived at her leisure
in comfort and pleasure.

One wall was dominated
by a large screen cable TV
upon which they could see
celebrities playing quiz games,
re-runs of sitcoms from long ago,
panel discussions by people who know
current events and
their own political agendum,
Hollywood movies, shop-at-home services
and infomercials for products at random.
There was an almost endless variety
of ordinary and marvelous
things that were shown,
trivia to be known
without ever leaving
the comfort zone
of chairs in which they sat
like regents on their thrones
in the company of laugh tracks
and canned applause
that helped to keep them
from feeling alone.

The Guardian was good natured
though his intelligence was crude,
and was so humbly respectful

that even when they made love
he never saw her nude.
She was scarcely aware
of the devotion and care
with which he fulfilled his chore
of always guarding the chamber door.

In this cozy fashion
many years did pass,
passionless as a clock,
colorless as a crystal glass.
Meanwhile the designs on the wall
had faded to a sickly pall.
The gold leaf had become drab
and the opals looked like scabs.
Some think it was the Guardian's
steaming eructations and breath
that lent the once brilliant walls
the obscure gray tedium of death.
But others know that features of being
when too familiar take flight from seeing
into the dull translucent film
of repetition's invisible realm.
Once concealed in colorless hues,
those features become primal ooze
that will slowly slosh and surge
until ugly little bordims emerge.
Bordims are just plain nasty fuckers
technically known as shadow suckers.
They are the Chamber's fatal flaw,
a dainty menace that will eat you raw.

So, having said that, without any further delay,
let's look in on our couple one fine day.

"Oh," she exclaims, "I'm so bored.
There is nothing to do, nothing at all.

Nothing is new, nothing at all."

And the subtle colorless forms in the wall
for just one moment swirl and sway.
Dropping to all fours,
the Guardian scampers across the floor.
In his eagerness to make everything right
the following poem he does recite:

"Calmness is good.
Excitement is bad.
You're the best girl
I've ever had."

"Actually," he confesses,
"you're the only girl I've ever had.
I guess that's what you call poetic license.
I hope it's not too daring
or that you don't think
I would ever lie.
I wish now I'd never said it!"
and he begins to cry.

"Be quiet," she says,
dressing him in garments of gold lame',
"Your poetry is sweet
in its own funny way."
Even as she assures him
that he is not too daring for her taste,
a little bordim slithers up on her
and begins to nibble and suck at her face.
"Oh!" she cries in great alarm,
"I thought you would protect me from all harm!"

"Indeed!" he shouts,
tearing the shadow from her features
and slamming it against the wall.

He stomps and slaps at every shadow
then turns to face her, standing tall.

"That sucker won't bother you any more,"
he does reassuringly speak.
But then he frowns and leans forward
to examine her ravaged cheek.
"Eww," he observes,
"that's gonna leave a nasty scar."

"Some protector," she sobs.
"I don't want to be here any more."

He groans, "But my darling,
there's no place else you can go."

She whispers through her tears,
"I know. Oh, I know."

Later she is brushing his baboon fur,
impulsively reaches out to stroke his beard.
He turns and as she looks at him and he at her,
Now suddenly arises,
constantly changing
in appearance and shape,
leaping across the Guardian's eyelid,
slithering in the light
like a fish in a lake,
peeping at her from whatever she sees,
brushing lightly against
her thighs and her knees,
licking her tongue and her teeth
and countless other teases,
seducing her in body and mind
and however else Now pleases.

Lowering her eyes, she cries,

"Leave me alone!
I hate how time flies!"

"What?" muttered the Guardian.

Now shows her how anything
to which she can cling
will hang onto her
like a ball and a chain,
plays the circumstances like a song
and suddenly as Now appeared
is exactly how swiftly Now is gone.

"What did you say?"
the Guardian asks,
reaching out to hold her hand.

"I can't tell you," she answers.
"There isn't a chance
that you'd understand."

Weeks pass in the chamber
like one long slow motion non-event.
She finds herself wondering
where Now came from
and where Now went.
As the Guardian fans his wings gently
and passes steaming farts of baboon scent,
she tells him about Now
as though it were something she dreamt.

The Guardian responds,
"I heard what you said,
but I really don't know
what you meant."

"Neither do I," she replies.

"It goes by so fast and means
everything while it's happening
and nothing at all when it's gone.
Now, it's gone."

And she suppresses a yawn.

Sometime later still
she's settled into her comfortable routine,
eating an apple and reading a magazine.
The Guardian is taking a snooze lying on his back
with wings wrapped around him
like a light sheet,
his feet sticking up in the air.
Suddenly a multitude of bordims attack,
swarming and sucking everywhere,
on her arms, her breasts, her face, in her hair!
Screaming, in a panic, she tears off her gown
and writhes naked on the floor.
"Oh!" She cries.
"These bordims are eating me alive!"
Guardian awakens with a roar,
destroying the bordims by tooth and by claw
until at last the battle is done.
Dead bordims are many.
But sense of victory, there is none.

She is lying on the floor,
sobbing and so distraught
that she doesn't give her nudity a thought.
But the Guardian, after years
of being devoted to duty,
is overcome at the sight
of her sensuous beauty.
He takes her hand
and his touching comes alive with physical elation
as he plays into the currents of feeling her sensation.

She becomes aware that in the past
in the night in the dark in their sex,
she was the one who had been dutiful.
As for the first time as he touches her,
too full of passion to apologize for his need,
she sees that he has always been beautiful.

For the first time she welcomes him
without wanting the deed to be over
before it's begun,
without faking half-hearted responses
while waiting for him to get done.
So for the first time
Now joins in their coupling.
As they kiss
Now is sipping at their lips,
a menage a trois as it were.
Now is her skin and Now is his fur.
She is almost entirely passive
while the Guardian
cries whispers in her ear
with his hands sliding
up and down her body
in a fury, like a storm.
As she receives
the Guardian's member
into her most private
sacred chamber of feeling,
(his first entrance here
without shyness),
Now pinches hard on both of her nipples
then dips a slippery finger
into her anus.
And the ecstatic sensual song
that she's held back all along
is finally released
in a melody of moans
and squeals

and joyful shrieks.
The Guardian is taken by surprise.
He does not realize that her screams,
whimpers and cries arise from the fact
that even as she and he engage
with abandon in the act of love,
she is gazing into the eyes of Now.

Is it a triad or a triangle?
It's hard to be exact
when definitions with words
come along after the fact.
Whatever we call this,
to her it's the same:
a starving ember in her womb
has burst into flame.
She never dreamed
it could be so exquisitely sweet
to trust each nuance of every
wiggle and thrust just as it's
choreographed by her own
irresistible bodily heat.
She is so hot with Now
that she can do no wrong.
Each movement fits with
perfection where it belongs.
The Guardian has slowed down,
their pleasure to prolong.
 Now is also moving so slowly
 as to almost be still.
 Yet her intensity keeps rising
 till her passion just boils over.
 She doesn't know how
 she can feel so much,
 experience so many
 dimensions of touch.
 She races over the edge. . .

The Guardian and Now absorb
and receive her excitement,
accelerating their movements till all three
attain momentary enlightenment.

When it's over but the delirium yet lingers,
the Guardian lies beside her,
massaging a nipple with his fingers.
For a moment she's at peace
till she feels the familiarity returning.
At the same time she is filled
with a most unfamiliar yearning.
She's drawn across the chamber
to a golden framed mirror.
She wants to see what she looks like,
wants to see if she's changed.
Until she looks in that glass she is not aware
that tears and sweat and baboon fur
have wiped away every trace
of makeup and color
from her body, hair and face.
For the first time in decades
she sees herself truly naked,
her gray hair sticking out in all directions.
Besides the other ravages of time,
she sees fresh and old scars of bordims
which appear as wrinkles, creases and lines.
For a moment she is silent
like a cat about to grasp its prey,
then she steps back,
looks down at her body in horror,
collapses on the floor
as though her bones had melted away
and she sobs out of control
over the Guardian's
bleating, concerned little lamb voice.
She is in an ecstasy of pain,

agony without choice.
She cries quietly a while
and then screams twice:
once out of anguish
and once out of rage.

In response,
the Guardian makes up a poem to recite:
"Knock! Knock! Who's there?
Why it's Mister Despair.
Just hold up your chin.
We won't let him in."

She looks at him in his human eyes,
strokes his baboon fur and then replies,
"This is not your fault. You're very sweet.
But it's time for me to go. I'm going to leave."
When the Guardian hears those words
he has no defense.

"You... you what?" he stammers,
looking to her like an angel
strangling on its own innocence.

"I'm going to leave," she repeats.

"You can't... I... What do you mean?"
as his eyes are pleading
please don't mean what I think.

"I'm going away! I'm going out the door and... "

"Out the door?!" he cries,
his voice breaking and baaing under the weight
of the unthinkable thought of being here alone.

"... and I won't be back!" she continues,

suddenly submerged in a tidal wave
of tears of her own.

"But how can I protect you?
I can't protect you if you go!"

"I know."
Her voice is swift and sharp
as a heart surgeon's scalpel making an incision.
"It's not up to you. This is my decision."

"No! No! No! I can't let you go!
I have to protect you.
As long as I'm alive, I can't let you leave."

"Then I'll have to kill you," she answers,
her voice taking on a hard, cutting edge.

"Your willingness to kill me kills me,"
he gasps, his heart bursting.
He falls over with blood
gushing out between his lips.
As he lies there dying,
with the very last breath
before he enters the realm of death,
he utters:
"Roses are red.
Violets are blue.
Till the end of time
I will love you."
He releases a tiny fart,
his wings twitch
and he is finally still.

"Poor darling Guardian," she sighs.
"It seems that you've left before me."
As she heads for the Chamber door

she thinks, *All of those years,*
every moment of every day,
instead of biding my time away,
I could have been
making love with Now!

As she passes through the Chamber door,
she's no longer attached to anything.
But it's far too late
for she's become
one of the screaming hags
of bitter fate.
And although in heaven
she's one of those persona non gratis,
by the extent of her suffering
she's earned immortal status
so that for the next thousand eons
that time does create
whenever lovers find they were dreaming
and that love did not wait
on the wind
on the river
in the empty sky
you can hear her sobbing and her crying
and her screams full of hate.
But she reserves her cackling, rueful laughter
for those fools who have traded their love
for the security of happily ever after.

Now or Never

Chapter 1

Wherever Never goes becomes the land that Never was, the land that has no sun. Where the dark moon is unseen (prowling like a black cat through the night). Where true delight has been forsaken or at least postponed. Where sighs set the stage for a false unknown.

Never is the ghost of a thief who died without ever being born, a sperm who finished last in the race to the ova, who doesn't understand that *this* contest is over.

Never slips past an invisible border into the world of Now. He grabs handfuls of scenery and flees back to his own realm. There he crouches in the darkness beneath a tree (a tree the seeds of which are eaten by birds before even one can touch the ground). Never examines the treasure he has found in a place that is no longer Now. The bright images in his hands are rapidly fading. He quickly whispers a magic spell:

"IF ONLY. . . IF ONLY. . . IF ONLY *THIS*. . ."

And the scenery responds so that a shadow on a leaf becomes a strand of his lover's hair. Sunlight on the earth turns into her face. The petals of a lilac form her lips as she leans toward him with her eyes closed, waiting for his kiss.

She expresses Never's longing to become more real. Her arms reach out of the disappearing moments he's managed to steal. Her face is ordinary, her body plain. Her personality a bit abrasive, but solid. Solid. Not so evasive as the static electricity of his own non-being. She lives outside his domain and resists all change. Everyone knows her as the Same.

The Same exists for Never just in his dreams. He exists for the Same exclusively in hers. So it is their sorry fate to meet only when they mutually masturbate.

Chapter 2

Same dwells in a world that Never should have been. She is part of the management team for a retail chain named Spenders Cellars. Spenders Cellars' shoppers glide up and down escalators with grim, glazed smiles beneath fluorescent lights. Credit cards nestled in wallets lubricate with desire while shoppers navigate a labyrinth of aisles. Colorful packaging, sale prices and merchandise displays dazzle the eyes, conspire to hypnotize each human being into parting with his or her legal tender, to surrender to the glitzy splendor of becoming a Spenders' spender.

Same has no time for fun and frivolity. For entertainment she's memorized every chapter and clause of Spenders International Corporate Policy. In her spare time she reads the work of economists who believe that all the world's needs can only be provided through corporate greed. She doesn't hesitate to employ every means she knows to preserve the status quo. She embodies the spirit of business as usual, practices the inverted magic of taking things for granted. She responds to innovation with friction and inertia. Entropy is her specialty. Her job title and her name are both The Same.

The part of her work she most enjoys is controlling everyone that Spenders employs. It's part of her job description to be easily annoyed. She snorts speed to remain skinny, quick and paranoid. Same instructs stock boys to be enthusiastic as they replenish the store's shelves, and not to talk among themselves. She is half crazed with the power to efficiently gauge if each hour they've worked hard enough to continue receiving minimum wage.

Cashiers get to be friendly. In fact, they're *required* to smile in the Spenders style they've been taught, and to be briskly cheerful but never to reveal a personal thought. Marketing came up with a script that began "Did you find everything you wanted?" This question works pretty well until a middle-aged overweight cashier named Lil asks it of an old man who stands at the till.

"Actually, no," he replies. "I'd hoped I would find true love and a meaningful life."

Lil begins laughing and can't stop even after the arrival of the cops who restrain her and take her away.

"Just goes to prove you can't be too careful what you say," **The Same explains at staff meeting next day.** "The script has been amended to read 'Did you find everything you need *here today?*'"

Throughout the next shift a cacophony of voices that are filtered through mandatory smiles drift up and down a dozen checkout aisles. "that you need"s mingle with "here today"s and "everything"s and "Did you find"s. This goes on until the laws of improbability have their fun and synchronize those voices (like JACKPOT lining up in every slot of a one-armed bandit). All at once the cashiers' voices rise up in unison like a Greek chorus, probing for the meaning of the life they are living. In the fleeting harmony it seems as though they are asking one another, "Did you find everything you needed *here today*?" And before a single customer can reply, twelve check out specialists begin to cry.

At last the script is modified to "Is there anything else you would like to buy?"

Although she gets paid very well and owns a lot of stuff, Same can see that she'll never be rich enough. Very late one night she realizes that most of the world's endless possibilities end up in the land that Never was. She admires the power of Never precisely so much as she longs to overcome him. She goes to him as a control freak speed freak dominatrix bitch. She entertains fantasies of B & D and S & M, imagines Never having to worry again, Never giving in to lust, pictures Never growing old, Never having to care and trust, yearns for Never feeling pain, Never fearing death, Never tasting one last breath, Never turning to bone and dust.

Never is overjoyed to accept *any* attention he can get because it makes him feel as though he exists. Whenever she invokes his name, she becomes his same old Same.

Chapter 3

Same is married to boring, predictable Linear Time but cheats on him with Never whenever she gets the chance. One night as she is watching the evening news, Linny slips out of his pants and shoes and takes her from behind with the measuring rod he wields like a god, taking his own thrill while demanding that she remain perfectly still. Quiet on the outside but screaming in her mind, she instantly consigns his every movement to Never, silently crying, *Never caress my skin! Never fondle my breast! Never bite my shoulder between extraction and thrust! Never come inside me!*

And Never does obey in his imaginary way. Thus it is that Same and Never (with a little help from Linny) conceive their only child.

Same is a fashion fanatic, a slave to style. One layer of lip gloss is the depth of her smile. She's in the powder room sniffing white powder and painting a face more fair upon her own when the infant miscarries, oozing out between her legs onto the red velvet cushion there. The Same is a tough one, definitely not a whiner and she finishes applying her eye liner before looking down. There she finds a cord umbilical, one end attached to a fetal belly the other disappearing into the mystery of her vagina. A quick snip of manicuring scissors and as she flushes baby down the toilet, she screams. At first it seems she is screaming to herself. "*Never keep this child! Never raise it as your own!*"

And Never does as he is told. The being he's received is not fully formed and has neither a gender nor an intention of its own. But Never is pleased that his child possesses substantial advantages *he's* never known, such as having been conceived and miscarried. Never's lack of physicality places him in a reality without beginning or end. From a peak of passion to which she'd momentarily climbed, Same had once called him "Never-Till-The-End-Of-Time". This infant on the other hand is mortal like its mother, borrowing substance from the future and past then disappearing with a gasp into the compost of that which does not last. And the name Same gives the child is When.

When is a trickster, a joker who is one part real, the other pretend, who loves to twist history into what it was not, to prophesy fictional situations in which real people get caught. When considers it a riot to be Never-The-Same as what anyone had thought.

Chapter 4

Linear Time invited Same to go for a walk with him. **"I think we should talk,"** he said, the corners of his mouth looking grim.

"My appointment book is full today," she replied, an excuse that usually got her off the hook.

"We'll do it right now," he retorted with a withering look.

There was nothing else that she could say. When Linny gave orders, The Same might resist but would always obey.

Together they strolled along the shoulder of the road that runs forever in a straight line between what is past and what will be in future time.

"The other day," he said, compressing his lips and creasing his brow, **"I took one of my business trips to a little place that exists half way between Never and Now."**

"Oh!" she exclaimed as though she'd been stung by a bug, then tried to conceal her reaction beneath a nonchalant shrug.

"There I met," he went on, **"the most androgynous being I ever did see. I still don't know if it was a he or a she. It kept shifting shapes and its eyes were wild. It claimed to be the unborn child of you and me."**

"No! Never!" she cried. "Inconceivable! Unbelievable!" In the bright sunlight she could see the enlarged pores on his nose. His arms were flapping with excitement, eyelid twitching, pupils contracted. His voice was still calm even though he otherwise had so visibly reacted.

He went on. **"This being disappeared for a moment then came back again and told me that its name is When."**

She tried to rush through that present moment. Her cheeks were hot and red as though on fire. "Everyone knows," she protested, "that When is a liar."

"I've also been given to understand," he shouted, **"that you and Never find comfort in each other's hands."**

"This is too much to bear!" **she sobbed.** "I never see Never. I never say Never."

"You lie," he whispered. **"Tell me the truth about you and When."**

Same glanced back over her shoulder toward the scenery they'd just passed. "*When* . . . when I was young," **she said,** "I was very pretty and thought it would last."

Far behind them, When appeared, at first looking like roadkill on the highway of time. Then flattened fur rippled in the wind, lifted itself and began dancing like an hallucinatory mime. The fur transformed into her hair. Some tire tracks tumbled into her features here and there. A bloody gash slipped into being her pouting lips. She was a pretty little girl indeed.

"Not *that* when!" Linny interrupted. **"That was before you were corrupted."**

She stopped and looked him straight in the eyes. "Should I be ashamed of who I am? Or of believing your lies? Or of being dumb? You stand as my accuser, but you're really the abuser who's made me into what I have become."

"Ours is a marriage of convenience," he hissed, **"and When is the child we promised each other."**

Her eyes bugged out and her mouth did gape. "What kind of child did you expect," **she demanded,** "from marital rape? Let me tell you what your lovemaking is to me. It's time you knew. You're just a pain in my old wazoo."

"Let's talk about you and When," he insisted.

For a moment she resisted then turned to him and said, "*When* . . . when I retire with the pension I've earned. . . "

Far ahead the street looked as though it had been paved with glass above which shimmered waves of heat. Sunlight refracted into its entourage of many colors, colors flowing into one another, becoming another made-by-When passing mirage.

The image they saw there was Same with grey hair sitting on the veranda of a villa in southern Spain.

Linny cried, **"No! Not that When either. Just tell me the truth about When and you!"**

"You don't care about the truth," she sneered. "You want me to spend my life chasing When ahead and dragging When behind and being blind to the fact that When is just a small-time act in the theater of the mind. When is a dream of what might have been."

Linny snorted and retorted, **"As though you wouldn't take any Whens you could find. Look, things aren't really all that deep. The bottom line is what you get paid and how much of it you get to keep."**

"If I could stop pretending about When," she mused, "I might feel pretty again."

"If you gave up on When, then you'd lose me too," Linear Time declared.

Same turned to him, stared and replied, "Lose you? I'm leaving you!"

"You *can't* leave me," Linny protested. **"It wouldn't make sense. You are always the Same. And I am the inevitable progression of events from one reality to the next."**

"Perhaps not so inevitable as you'd have me believe. Instead of endless pointless endeavor, instead of you or Never, what if I chose to be in the here and now?"

"Right!" Linny responded with a snicker.

"I'm sick of saying 'yes' to 'no'. I'll never get to come until I go. Tears have washed the makeup from my face! Now, how do I get out of this place??!!"

"You're standing too close to see me," Now whispers in reply. "Take a step back. Take a deep breath."

What Same sees when she slips inside the present moment gives her a bigger rush than a nose full of meth. Clouds are drifting across the sky. There are leaves and birds moving in the trees. Her skin is being kissed by a summer breeze.

Blue wildflowers are trembling with delight in the swaying grass. Iridescent purple dragonflies hover nearby and look at her with compound eyes.

"One moment here is worth more than a lifetime in Spenders!" she sighs.

Linny couldn't find a way to get into Now. He ran back and forth and all around, angrily and futilely demanding her attention. **"Same, come back!"** he cried. **"You've got to come back to your senses."**

She giggles and says, "I just did."

Interlude

. "Memories are the shadows of a bird in flight. Memories are dreams of an angel with no past. Memories are precious artifacts of change."

Adrienne, *The Last Dragon*

"I could not be consoled by knowing it was fate nor by the endless mystery of creation nor by the former glories of our race."

The Last Dragon

Chapter 1: *The Dragon's Tale*

My analyst suggested that besides Deep Breathing Meditation classes, I should take a nature walk at least once a week. So I drove out to the so-called Endless Forest. There I followed a narrow trail that passed through a small grove. And in that grove was an old blind man who was pretending he could see. He was poking ahead of each hesitant step with a wooden staff, wandering in circles trying to find the path. The moment I entered the clearing he abruptly stopped, leaned nonchalantly on the walking stick and said "Hello?"

"Good afternoon," I responded.

"Are you lost?" he asked.

"Oh, no," I laughed. "I'm just out for a walk in the woods to soothe my nerves."

"Good," the old man replied and walked jauntily toward me. He casually touched the ground just once with his staff and actually twirled it like a dancer with a baton. He stopped a few feet from me. He looked as though he were wearing contact lenses of a translucent milky gray. He gazed in the direction where he imagined my face to be. "Do you know where the main camp is?" he asked.

I told him I'd passed through it not half an hour before. His face twitched toward my voice. "Very good," he said. "I'll show you how to get back there so you don't lose your way."

I had to smile as I agreed. He took a couple of steps closer, leaned toward me and very quietly said, "I have something that you might need."

When I inquired what that might be, he stepped even closer. He raised his eyebrows and whispered, "If you give me everything you own and agree to abandon all human pleasure, I'd be willing to teach you about the Dragons' Treasure."

When I declined, he was quick to say, "Well then, never mind. Just head for the main camp and I'll let you know if you turn the wrong way."

He followed the sound of my footsteps as we walked. After a while, he stopped me and said, "My name is Adrienne and I am the last dragon. I have assumed human form for reasons I shall presently relate. How wretched and blessed is this mortal state. One becomes old in less than a blink of eternity's eye. Your pleasures and torments are so sweet and fierce and fleeting and then you die. As so shall I. Indeed *soon* shall I."

The old man's demeanor had become sullen.

"You see," he said, "I burst out of my egg into an explosion of light more than ten billion years ago. And even though I was born just that instant, I already knew more than any of your race shall ever dream. I knew my lineage back to the beginnings of time and that I was to be the last dragon. I was one with the fires of countless suns, was the dimensionality of space through which celestial bodies spun. This planet was little more than a speck of dust that I watched form when I was still young but had chosen death over being alone."

"Why were you alone?" I asked. "Where were your mother and father, your uncles, aunts and cousins, not to mention all the others of your kind?"

Adrienne laughed a bitter laugh. "You obviously know little about the dragon's estate. Unlike humans, we do not proliferate into countless individuals, each knowing only it's own self as though it were separate from the species whole. There was but one male dragon and one female at any particular time. Ahhh, and when these two mated . . . when we mated, we lingered in every nanosecond as though it were frozen in time, penetrating and receiving at every point of every plane of every cell of our beings. Thus we danced as one for billions of years till only the purest nature of male and female dragon-ness remained. When release at last came, it flung us to opposite sides of the universe where we each turned white hot and melted into the stone eggs out of which the next two dragons would emerge."

"What an astonishing metaphor!" I exclaimed.

"It's not a metaphor, you fool!" Adrienne had begun to weep. "It's the naked face of truth! Except it never again will be. I waited millennia to hear her mating song telepathically blowing in the cosmic winds. When the invitation didn't come, I went off to search for her. I flew over craters and mountains on distant planets both sides of the caves you call black holes. When at last I found her egg, it was silent within and on the outside cold. I could not be consoled by knowing it was fate nor by the endless mystery of creation nor by the former glories of our race."

Tears now covered the old man's face. He swiped at them with his sleeve, then continued, "I languished in profound misery at the edge of a galaxy and watched life on this planet evolve to the human pattern. I had to wait through humanity's hundred-thousand years of primitive fruitarian bliss, then through twenty-five-thousand years of ice age while you lived in caves and learned to kill animals for their hides and flesh. I waited still."

"Do you mind if I inquire what you were waiting for?" I asked.

"As the last of my race I could not end my days until there was a species that had developed enough language skill and science to receive and keep the Dragons' Treasure."

"I see," I responded.

"When people discovered the curse of iron, I knew my time was drawing near. Soon there was machinery and greed and the pathetic mythology of heroes who overcome evil by violent means. I had only to dwell in misery a few thousand years more until some of mankind would be ready for my gift. At last, not even a century ago, the time was right. In the heart of night I practiced the dragon equivalent of masturbation, imagining the sensations of merging with my non-existent mate. At the peak moment of poignant desolate ecstasy, without a thought of waiting, I resolved my entire essence into the life force of a single sperm that was at that instant attaining union within the womb of a human woman who was ovulating. Thus as a mortal being was I born."

"So then," I interjected, "it was not just to end being alone that you joined the human race?"

"No, no!" Adrienne replied with a sigh. "I became human so that I could pass on the Dragons' Treasure and thus be free to die. For a dragon, entering mortality is a very swift form of suicide."

The old man moaned and, leaning on his walking staff, said, "You haven't even heard the most bitter part of my ordeal. It happened when I'd been on the earth for seventy-one years. I awoke one morning with her telepathic love song overflowing my human brain. She was calling me in tones of abandoned passion, longing for my touch as a drought struck land waits for rain. I was scarcely able to bring myself to answer, to tell her what I'd done." He sighed and drifted off into silence.

I asked, "What did she say then?"

"Oh," he finally answered, "hours went by before she replied. Her voice had the timbre of a skyscraper crumbling in an earthquake as she cried, *'Why didn't you wait?'*

Through my tears I responded, *'Why were you so late?'"*

"Did she tell you?"

"No, she said she wanted to follow me here. I explained that if she did, the most that would be gained would be for her as a small child to watch me suffer the indignities and pain of reaching such an advanced age for a man before I died."

Standing there at the old man's side, I turned away while he cried. At last Adrienne continued, "She sank into the anguish and rage that never passes, there to burst into flame and thus remain till nothing was left of her but ashes."

Chapter 2 *The Leash of Time*

As he told the tale of the last dragon, Adrienne's pale thin features flitted through a variety of transformations. At one moment he seemed merely very old and very wretched. In another instant, his visage appeared to be that of a noble mythic hero, the gray cataracts floating in his eyes a brilliant artistic brush-stroke of the tragic. Humble suffering and fierce pride gave away at times to the tenderness of a frail poet or the flair and style of a mime. All this as he moved me near to tears with his story.

In the silence that followed the disastrous ending of his narrative, my apprehension of him likewise passed through a rapid series of changes. I wondered if he was psychotic or a new-age con man hawking his Dragons' Treasure. Then it seemed clear he was both at once, an insane pitchman for his own cosmic carnival. Yet his performance was incredibly inspired and his fairy tale was tinged with the profound. I was entirely unconvinced, of course, but fascinated. In a way, I guess I was hooked.

We were walking again through the forest. Neither of us had uttered a word since the story ended. The path became narrower and I pulled back the limbs of bushes so they wouldn't get in his face. Finally I stopped and turned to him. He halted also and directed a curious sightless gaze toward me. "So, okay. What's this Dragons' Treasure thing?" I asked. "Is there anything tangible to it at all? Is it a cult or philosophy or religion? Some kind of doctrine or meditation or prayer?"

"No," he shook his head sadly. "None of the above." He then began nodding his head vigorously while the corners of his lips twitched toward a smile. "And," he exclaimed, "all of the above! And so much more!" His face opened into a grin of childish delight. "It's the seeing of Seeing! It's being Being!" He cackled and laughed. He was having a good old time. "It's the appearing-disappearing act that goes on forever!" He released one last chuckle and became very sober once more. Scowling, his voice deepened into the vibrato of reverb as he pronounced, "The Dragons' Treasure is awakening to who you really are and always have been." He seemed to deflate and shook his head as he had before. "It's experiencing without measure. No, it's not easy to describe the Dragons' Treasure."

"Well, what is it exactly that you're selling at such an unpayable price?"

"Unpayable price?" he sneered. "Huh! Just forget it. Let's get back to the camp. I want to take a nap."

As we tramped on, the silence was penetrated by mews of a catbird and by the shhhh of a breeze. My footsteps also must have made some sound which Adrienne followed gracefully as if he could see. He was one of the most intriguing characters I'd met. Of course his story was a delusion and the Dragons' Treasure no more than a colorful scam. But when I tried to think of some other topic to draw him out, my mind felt like it was grasping at empty air. At last I said over my shoulder, "I've got a couple hundred dollars in my pocket. It's all I have with me. But it's yours for the asking. You can probably use it more than me."

"Stop and look at me," Adrienne replied.

I did.

"Do I look like I need your money?" he gently demanded while his lips pouted.

For the first time I noticed that, although soiled and stained, his shirt and trousers were hand made. Thin cashmere wool. Finely woven cotton. On his left hand he wore a red gold ring that bore an emerald large enough to befit a king. All I could say was, "I apologize. I didn't mean to offend you."

His voice was patient, his face the face of kindness as he inquired, "What is it you want?"

"I don't know," I answered. "Maybe a sneak preview, like a movie trailer, of whatever this is you call the Dragons' Treasure."

He closed his eyes and reflected a moment, then opened them again as though he were going to comply. Instead he asked me, "Why?"

My answer was a shrug, which I immediately realized he couldn't see. "Idle curiosity," I said. "Maybe just killing time."

"I'd advise you to take your curiosity out of idle and put it into gear. Killing time is serious business here. Sorry, no free samples. Let's be on our way."

"In other words, just to find out what you're talking about would cost all I have or could ever desire?"

"Yes, yes," he responded wearily. "Now can we please get back to the camp?"

"Not yet." I was becoming a little irritated. "What if someone *did* give you everything and then decided your treasure wasn't worth it?"

"He doesn't pay me till after."

His answer took me aback a bit. I hesitated. "Well, suppose he paid you and then the treasure didn't last?"

He flashed me a mysterious smile. "What if Eternity doesn't last?"

"I don't know much about Eternity," I responded. "Being merely human, I've never experienced it."

He wagged a finger at my face. His voice filled with exasperation, he asked, "What do you think you're experiencing now?"

"Bewilderment," I replied.

He laughed. "Bewilderment is fine. It's definitely better than being sure of some opinion. Anyhow, right now is forever."

I began laughing too. "Your mean for millions of years I'm going to have to listen to you saying that now is forever?"

We were laughing together, like a scene out of some sort of metaphysical buddy movie. I said, "What's scary is that sometimes I think I half understand some of what you're saying."

He abruptly stopped chuckling and seemed to become quite dejected. "What I'm saying isn't the point," he muttered. Suddenly he snapped his fingers in the air and broke into an endearing grin. "It isn't the point. It's the pointer!"

"Now you've lost me again," I complained. "This time completely."

"Right now is forever," he repeated in a whisper. "There's never been another moment. Not one other moment. There's never been any other day."

"Yeah, right," I replied. "All those watches and clocks and calendars and appointment books are merely for decoration."

"Listen now," he earnestly commanded. "Clock time is an attempt to synchronize the constantly changing perceptions of a multitude of dreamers. It's the job description for drones that produce and consume in a society of delusions."

"That's preposterous!" I cried. "You're saying that time doesn't exist!"

"No," he insisted. "I'm saying you've got all the time there is in the world right now."

"What about the seconds that keep going past?" I asked. "The minutes, hours, days and years?"

"If you subtract all the particulars that make a moment real," he was enunciating each word distinctly, "you can break up the imaginary empty nothing that's left into constant intervals. Make timepieces to keep everyone in step. Do you call *that* reality?"

"So you're saying that linear time is nothing more than a paradigm?"

"Right now is the ultimate moment," he replied. "It's the home sweet home you've never left and to which you can never return. The price of quantifying life is quality of life. Head for the orgasm, miss the lovemaking. It's the modern way."

"This isn't just a concept?" I asked, slightly amazed. "You believe there's really some other way to look at time?"

He replied in a sing-song voice, almost a chant. "No matter how fast the human creature spins around, it never has found nor will ever find a single still frame lingering behind. Thus, objective history is unmasked as illusion. Memories are the shadows of a bird in flight. Memories are dreams of an angel with no past. Memories are precious artifacts of change."

"So," I sighed. "This, at last, is the Dragons' Treasure."

Adrienne responded to my comment as though I'd just made the ultimate joke. He laughed till he was choking on his own laughter. His face turned bright red. For a moment I considered the Heimlich Maneuver. He finished the outburst with a sneeze, wiped his nose with a cashmere sleeve and wheezed, "No, my boy. This is not the Dragons' Treasure. It's no more than taking off time's leash while you're still in the cage of your own confusion. But it's a necessary first step in the right direction."

"If linear time is the leash," I asked in mild alarm, "then what is the cage?"

Adrienne hesitated, knowing he was about to tell me something I really didn't want to hear. He stuck an index finger in his right ear and twisted it as though cleaning out some wax. Then he took a step closer, got right in my face and said in a hoarse voice, "All your opinions and everything you believe."

"Oh?" I giggled nervously. "Is that all?"

"Yes. Nothing you can possibly think about reality is reality. It's just a thought till you invest in it with belief. Then it becomes your cage."

"Okay, this is enough!" I exclaimed. "I don't understand your treasure and I'm not going to go there! You want me to leave everything that's familiar behind. I don't think so! You're trying to take me somewhere that's weird and completely unknown. Somehow, I find that terrifying."

"Yes," he responded. "Fear is definitely the lock on the door to the cage."

"If I gave up time and everything I believe is true, I don't know how I'd survive!" I protested.

He held up the same finger with which he'd picked his ear. "Does a tiger living in a zoo think the jungle's too dangerous?" he asked.

"I don't know," I reacted. I could hear the desperation in my own voice. "Yes! I bet he does!"

Adrienne grinned at me. "Turn him loose! See how quickly he changes his mind!"

Chapter 3 *Cage of Illusions*

The woods opened into a clearing with a river passing through it. The path continued across a bridge.

"Wait," called Adrienne from behind me. "Do you hear that? We'll soon come to the stream that runs through the Endless Forest."

"Yes, I know," I replied. "In fact, we're there already."

"There's a little concrete bridge that crosses the stream," he went on.

"Yes," I replied. "I see it now."

"Good." He nodded with a satisfied smile. "We're getting close to the camp. I'll be glad to get to my tent. Are you set up there too?"

"No," I told him. "I just came for the day."

"You should stay longer sometimes," he said. "When you've lived immersed in nature for a while, you won't want to go back to the city."

"Suburbs," I said.

"Whatever," he replied. "Ahhh. Let's rest on this bridge a few moments. I love the sound the river makes." He leaned on the railing and took a deep breath. In his face I could see both his physical frailty and the strength of his spirit. I realized that in a very short time, I'd formed a deep affection for this man.

Giving me a sidelong glance as though he could see, he said, "You know what you're afraid of is your own world, your birthright. When you try to run from it, it's even the running. There's no way that's away."

"I don't want to talk about it," I whispered.

"Alright," he mumbled. "Alright. Okay. Instead, would you like to know more about the history of dragons?"

"Yes, in fact I would," I replied eagerly. "Please tell me. I'm all ears."

"Once," he began, "there were a thousand dragons living at the center of this planet and I was one of them."

"No!" I cried in indignation. "Not an hour ago you told me there was only one male and one female dragon alive at any time. And you were on the edge of the galaxy . . . "

"Quiet!" he interrupted. For just an instant he gave me an enraged frown, then he relaxed his face into nothing less than a friendly grin. "As I was saying, a thousand of us lived in the middle of the earth. Each of us was at the heart of the others' being. Oceans formed on the world's surface from the mist of our tears. Diamonds coalesced wherever we exhaled the flame of breath. Rock mantles and platelets of the earth's crust shifted at the weight of our steps. Human-generated nuclear bombs would have been less than a spark in the solar explosions of our dreams. All this happened before your time."

"No! No!" I shook my head. "I don't want to hear any more!"

"If you'd like to be realistic," he said, "then the first cue is for your perspective to accommodate more than one view."

"No!" I protested. "I've heard enough lies in my life. I don't need more confusion."

"Ahhh," he sighed and smiled. "Then you may be ready for a lesson concerning the illusion of truth and the truth of illusion."

"No! I don't think so!" I vehemently responded. "I never agreed to do this Dragons' Treasure thing. Forget about it! I'm done! Please! Don't say anything else about it!"

"All right." His voice was conciliatory. "But why are you so upset?"

"I'm not upset!" I snapped. I took a deep breath and closed my eyes, remembered to be calm. "I guess I got my hopes up about something. I don't even know what."

"Don't worry about it," he said. "What you forgive is what you forget."

"What's that supposed to mean?" I demanded, edgy as a slippery precipice.

"Nothing," he responded. "Forget it. My fault really. I'm not always coherent. Sometimes I ramble."

I closed my eyes again and practiced deep breathing with a silent Om. At last, I looked again at Adrienne. What a pathetic, preposterous, mysterious old man! I realized that he would soon be out of my life, that I'd probably never see him again. "Sorry I got so emotional," I said.

"No problem," he graciously replied. "I'm only here to bare the secret for those who can bear it. If you're unable, that's just how it is."

Gazing at him, I realized my regret was not just for the loss of his companionship. It didn't matter that he sometimes lied. He'd hinted at a way of seeing that reminded me of . . . something. I couldn't recall what. He was in touch with a world I lost when I was a child. "I'm sorry," I repeated. "I just got sort of nervous and afraid. Like what you said about the lock on the cage."

"I understand," he replied. His face almost drooped with looking so sad.

"Listen," I said. "I think we might go a little further if you'll let me control the pace."

"How would we do that?" His tone was mild and resigned.

"I'll ask you questions," I said. " If your answers upset me, we stop. Then I'll ask another question when and if I'm ready."

"I think I might agree to that," he replied. "What would be the first question you'd ask?"

I thought about it. "Karma," I finally said. "I think the subject of Karma might be pretty safe. Tell me about Karma."

"Do you want to know about Karma, the reality?" he inquired. "Or the word?"

"The reality," I responded without hesitation.

"Karma," he said in a casual, conversational way, "is very simply that you create the world in which you must live with every thought or deed or word you say."

"What? Me? I create the world?"

He smiled. "Not exclusively. It's kind of a group effort. You collaborate with everyone you know or see or love or hate."

"That's it? That's all?"

He chewed on his lower lip a bit, then replied, "Oh, let me give you one example. If you believe you live in a dog-eat-dog world, then you do. What you give is what you get. I could say much more. But that's all you really need to know for now."

"Then," I asked, "what about Karma, the word?"

"I'm afraid the word has fallen into the hands of moralists," he answered matter-of-factly. "They make Karma into a guilt trip or an ego trip because that's all they know."

"Why?" I asked. "Why would that be so?"

"Well," he replied, "I'm sure you realize that truth stands apart from punishment and reward. Reality's not some omniscient Santa or malevolent Satan. The losses and gains of a dream disappear the moment you awaken."

"So you think good Karma and bad Karma are variations on the theme of heaven and hell?"

He sang to me, "*He knows if you've been bad or good, so be good for goodness' sake.*"

"I think we'd better stop," I told him. "I'm getting nervous again."

"Your choice," he replied. "But would you mind if I say one more thing? Just to clarify what's already been said?"

"It may be the clarity that's scary," I replied. "But go ahead."

"If you want to train an animal to perform tricks, you use a whip and a carrot on a stick. If you'd like someone to contemplate truth you use neither. Once a human has completed that kind of training, there's not a lot of truth remaining. He doesn't question what he's been told, because he dare not risk it. A wolf dreams of chasing rabbits. A poodle dreams of a pat on the head and a biscuit."

"Okay, that's enough!" I declared. "Let's give it a rest."

"Fine," he said, turning his head away quickly so that I might not see his mischievous grin. It was late afternoon and not particularly warm but I was sweating. "What a very pleasant breeze," he commented, turning his face to me again. And it was. The thin white hair that barely covered his head rippled in the air. The stubble on his cheeks and chin stood out in the fading light of the sun. I wouldn't mind looking like him when I get old.

"Tell me a little about your human life," I requested. "Do you mind if I ask your age?"

"I turned ninety-seven in the spring," he replied. "Still have a few years left in me."

"What were your human parents like?" I wanted to know.

"My parents? Alright," he said. "When my Mom was young, she was a stripper in a bordello. A former courtesan, she liked to say. She earned a fortune and invested it well. Oh, but the side she knew of human nature made her bitter."

"And your father?" I asked.

"Dad. He sold corsets before becoming a major league sports outfitter." he replied. "He was generous but stern and loved to learn. He was a millionaire many times over."

"Was your family close?" I inquired.

"I guess so," he responded. "In his later years, Dad acquired a football team. Sometimes we all traveled together to watch them lose. We lived in estates scattered all over the world and every winter we'd take a Caribbean cruise."

"Life of luxury," I commented.

"That's true," he agreed. "There was never anything I could need that wasn't given before I would ask. Except respect. At the age of five I began at last trying to articulate about my dragon past. They praised my imagination and said I was cute. Don't know what I expected from a clothing merchant and an ex-prostitute. They died without knowing who I am" For a moment the look on his face was a portrait of bitterness. That expression faded into sorrow as he added with a sigh, "And they never saw who they, themselves, truly were."

"So, tell me. . . how and when did you first realize you were a dragon?" I asked.

He frowned, not unpleasantly but in disbelief that I would ask a such a foolish question. "I was born knowing I was the last dragon, of course. When did you first realize you were you?"

"I don't know," I replied. "Seems far back as I can remember, I've always been me." Then I had to laugh nervously, compulsively. Suddenly I was back in the clammy, clumsy grip of self-consciousness. Wriggling to get loose, I said, "The reflections on the river are beautiful. Of the clouds and the trees." As I uttered this, the water's surface parted and a trout dispersed some clouds in a lazy swirl of iridescent colors. I blurted out, "I just saw a fish!"

"In reality are there clouds and trees on the river's skin?" he asked.

"What do you mean?" I responded. "Yes, there are reflections."

"But the reflections are an illusion, aren't they?"

"I guess so. Like a mirror."

"When a sign of the life that lives and breathes beneath the illusion arose, were you disturbed?"

"No," I answered. "It kind of gave me a thrill."

"And so it should," he muttered. Once again, he turned his head away.

His words were oddly reassuring. "Well," I heard myself say, "then I guess I'll ask another question."

"I'm ready," he was quick to reply.

"This," I asserted "is *the* big question. I'm going to try very hard not to over-react, no matter what you come up with." He nodded his head. I continued. "Some contend that the random chaos of causes and effects has produced the entire universe, right down to this conversation. Others say that some divine Intelligence has created all this, including us. What's your view?"

"Ah, yes," he responded immediately. "The old dumb and dumber debate."

"Alright!" I cried out in anger. "This time you've gone too far! You dishonor all religion and all science in a single breath!"

"No, I don't," he mildly replied.

"Oh yes, you do!" I practically screamed in his face.

"No," he spoke very quietly. "I dishonor heartless technology and mindless theology in a single breath."

"One or the other has to be right!" I insisted. "It's either a big accident or it's made by God!"

"Offhand, I can think of many other possibilities," he replied.

"Name one!" I demanded.

"Oh, I'll give you several." With these words, he laid down the staff, took a step backward and began a little routine like a street performer who's been through this a thousand times before.

Directing a slight bow in my direction, he said, "What if both sides are right"? He raised his hands toward the sky. "And it's the will of God for the universe to arise randomly out of the laws of nature He's ordained?"

He gave me a moment to contemplate that thought, then asked, "Or what if both sides are wrong?" He leaned over, shaking both his hands toward the ground as though he were trying to get something off his skin. "And what if it's our own intelligence in apprehending the laws of nature that is Divine?"

Again he paused. Then with a look of amazement on his face, he began jerking his head from place to place. "Or what if there are multitudes of deities, as so many cultures believe? A different God for every occasion?"

Another little delay and he blinked his eyes rapidly at me, eyebrows raised as though in awe. "Or what if this is all a dream *you're* making up as you go along?"

A couple seconds later he shrugged, turned and walked a few steps away. "What if God is not a He but a She or a Both or a Neither or is totally beyond our comprehension?" he asked over his shoulder. He turned to face me and continued, "And what if the universe is continuously creating itself by destruction and destroying itself by creation?"

He waited. Then with perfect timing and grace, brought his hands together and clasped them tenderly over his heart. "Or what if immutable physical laws and ineffable perceptual processes work hand in hand to manifest it all?

A long pause this time. At last he raised both arms straight over his head and very slowly sank cross legged to the ground. "Or what if there is one infinite Consciousness that by it's nature forever descends from the ether to solid matter, implanting Its divine awareness into every living thing?" He began laughing. He sat there laughing and laughing and laughing.

Finally he sobered and shook his head then his finger at me, like a kind parent gently scolding a child. "What if the believers in all these possibilities joined the dumb and dumber debate? What if each of them was right about something and wrong about denying what was right in the others' views? All the believers talking and no one listening to anyone but themselves? What do I mean 'what if'? That *is* what's happening, isn't it? Or maybe not. I guess it's all open to interpretation."

At last the nervousness was gone. I was positively exhilarated. "I didn't realize so many viewpoints were possible."

"Oh, I could go on and on." He smiled. "I was just getting started. My own personal favorite is one I made up myself. I call it The Principle of Ephemera. Want to hear it?"

"Sure," I replied. "Go ahead."

"Let's suppose we live in a universe named Space. Besides its own three-dimensionality, the primary characteristic of Space is Motion. Motion permeates Space everywhere in the universe, even where there is no object to move, not one photon to be found. Are you with me so far?"

"No," I answered. "How can there be movement when there's nothing to be moving?"

"Good question." He gave me an encouraging smile. "The intersection of Space and Motion is a continuity called Now. Now is always everywhere, but is never anywhere twice the same."

"I'm afraid I'm lost again."

"Let me put it this way. Artists grab at fragments of Now, but it's like trying to take home the river in a cup. Lovers enter Now doggie fashion, missionary position or upside-down. Now entertains the masses with mass in motion in extreme disguise. If all sentient beings were fish, Now would be the ocean that surrounds them as well as the ocean in each one's eyes."

Although I only dimly got his meaning, a little chill ran up my spine. "What did you say you call this?" I asked. "The Principle of . . . what?"

"Oh," he replied, "I also call it The Dragons' Treasure."

"*That's* the Dragons' Treasure?" I cried with a squeal.

"Of course not!" he retorted almost in anger. "It's just some words about it. You must learn to distinguish between words and what's real."

I reacted with indignation. "Don't you know how to talk without self-contradiction?" I demanded. "Can't you just tell me what the Dragons' Treasure really is?"

He shook his head and shrugged. "Anything I can say is only more words."

"So what's wrong with that?" I insisted. "There's nothing wrong with words!"

"You're right," he stated. "Words do have their place. But the words 'she smiled' are not the same as the expression that passes once across someone's face."

"Come on," I whined. "Just spit it out. Is there such a thing as the Dragon's Treasure or not?"

The look on his face turned sour. "Words can't get you there," he said. "You'll have to go the rest of the way on your own power."

"Power?" I had to sneer and laugh. "I'm a Senior Data Management Engineer. The only power I have is to hire or fire office staff. And I'm not even good at doing that."

"Delegated authority isn't power," he sniffed.

"Then I have no power at all!" I cried. "None!"

"Yes you do." He gave me a smile that came fast, didn't last and ended with a frown. "Power isn't circumstance either. It's what you do with circumstance. That's the Dragon's Treasure, the power with which you were born."

"Suppose I feel helpless?" I asked.

"Yes," he replied in a gentle voice. "That's what you're doing with your power. That's your choice."

"It's not what I want to choose!" I cried. "How do I change my mind?"

"Relax," he said. "It's never too soon or too late. Whatever you direct your attention to, you activate."

118

I didn't understand and stared at him blankly.

Adrienne continued, "If you appreciate Beauty, she'll give you her key and invite you to her place." He gave me a thumbs up. "Or. . . if you get busy demonizing other people, then don't be surprised when a bunch of angry demons get in your face."

"Okay, I see that," I responded. "But how do I start?"

"Just take in the Everything all around you," he replied. "Go with it wherever you want to go. That's how you'll discover the Dragons' Treasure."

I sat down next to him beside the bridge and began deep breathing again. I could feel my heart powerfully, rhythmically contracting and expanding nestled near the bellows of my lungs. A breeze of fresh air washed up on my face and hands like water on the shore. The setting sun spread a warm orange glow everywhere. My nostrils dilating, skin tingling, I watched a dragonfly catch gnats in the air. I whispered to Adrienne, "I've got it!"

What started as a small smile at the edges of Adrienne's lips quickly spread to his whole face. "Good," he said. "You might like to know, you are the twelfth person ever to tell me so."

In a state of surrender, I murmured, "I guess now I'm supposed to give you all I own."

He laughed and said, "Forget it. I tell people that just to separate the wheat from the chaff. Anyone who doesn't prefer Truth to possessions or pleasure simply can't see the Dragons' Treasure."

Chapter 4 *Reunion*

"So what happens now?" I asked.

Adrienne made a funny face, the silly grin of a clown with eyebrows raised high, and answered, "You live happily ever after."

"No, I don't," I laughed. "I've always despised happy endings. They're so goopy."

"Hidden in the end of every ending is the beginning of something new. So how about good beginnings?" he inquired with a smile.

"Yeah," I replied. "That sounds a little better. You say this awareness lasts indefinitely?"

"Oh, it's like a strobe light. You lose it and find it again and again. That's *how* it lasts."

"I really don't want to go back to the confusion and suffering," I told him.

"Suffering is pathos," he said. "Without it, shallowness would be your mark as an artist. Inanity would be your character as a work of art."

"What about the confusion?" I asked.

"Most confusion comes from believing or disbelieving what you've been told," he answered. "Some of it's the by-product of attempting to get what you think you want. The rest arises out of trying to avoid suffering. Whenever you get distracted from what's happening in the Now, you get confused."

There was nothing more I could think of to say. The full moon had come up. enormous and translucent, before the sun went down. The river voiced a constant rippling whisper as Adrienne and I sat beside the bridge. Textures seemed magnified. Supple veined leaves trembled in the trees. Stones squatted, smooth and mottled in the grass. Vaporous wisps detached and dispersed from the edges of cumulous clouds. A coarse tree root protruded out of moist black earth. Some sort of enchantment prevailed. Everything seemed familiar, like coming home after a long time away. The air was breathing in my ear. I laughed a little. "That breeze," I said to Adrienne, "sounds almost like a lover's breath."

He replied, "Or like a woman's voice calling from very far away."

I listened. "Now that you mention it," I said. "the breeze does sound more and more like a woman."

We fell silent again.

"Wait!" Adrienne jumped to his feet. He turned his head this way and that. "It *is* a woman's voice!" he exclaimed. "Listen! She's calling!" I couldn't imagine why he was so excited.

Moment by moment the voice became more distinct. "It sounds like she's crying out something in a foreign language," I finally said.

"What?" he prompted me. "What does it sound like she's saying?"

"Sounds like 'shoe in yada'," I replied.

Adrienne was now poised like an explorer who's just reached the top of a mountain. He said, "Shoon-Yata is my dragon name. There's only one who could know it!"

Far down the path on the other side of the bridge, I could see a woman approaching. She saw us too and broke into a swift graceful run. "Shoon-Yata! It's you!" she cried. She ran to him, took his cheeks in her hands and peered into his unseeing, tear-filled eyes. She was Asian, in her mid-twenties and sensuous as a cat. Wordlessly, her lips articulated the body's exquisite language for tenderness, relief, anguish and joy. Her nostrils flared. Dense dark lashes surrounded her amber eyes . Those eyes radiated delight that would eclipse all sorrow. Lucky Adrienne. She was the most beautiful woman I'd ever seen.

"Dar-Shan," he said, his voice resonating deep and somber. "I thought you were dead."

"I exercised the feminine prerogative," she replied playfully. "I changed my mind."

"Why didn't you call?" he asked with a pained whine.

"As a human I'd lost my dragon powers, including telepathy," she answered. "But when I faced in your direction, I could feel a warm tingle all over my skin. Even three continents away. Ten years ago I left my parents and began following that tingle. I had no idea of how far away you might be or how long it would take. I just knew I had to find my precious, only Shoon-Yata."

"If I'd known you were here. . . " he began, then put his arms around her.

She gasped. Her eyes opened even wider. "Soon as you embraced me," she said, "my telepathy came back."

"So I noticed," he replied, his voice husky and his breathing loud. "And my vision seems to be returning. I clearly see a dim shadow where you're standing. A moment ago it was entirely dark."

Involuntarily I screamed, "I hate happy endings!!!" I don't think either of them heard me or even knew I was there.

"Do you know what I'm doing now?" she asked, removing her blouse, full nipple-tipped breasts exuberant in the pastel crepuscular light.

"You seem to be dancing," he replied.

"I'm taking off all my clothes," she happily stated. "Do you like the human female form?"

"Oh, yes," he responded. "It's so accommodating to human maleness." With each breath, Adrienne seemed to become more manly. His shoulders seemed broader and his chest expanded. His features became bolder and more distinct.

She was entirely naked now and rubbed full body against him, saying, "Here. Let me help you remove your shirt."

I decided it was time for me to leave and walked away quickly. Behind me, I could still hear the melodic murmurings of her impetuous laughter and the bold intonations of his voice.

I heard Adrienne moan. It was the moan of a man in love as he enters his lover for the first time. It was a long moan that began quietly and gradually grew louder till it rumbled like thunder, then rushed in a warm roar against my back. I stumbled forward as the wave of explosion transformed into a hiss which ascended into silence. I looked up to see that the sky was black. Sun, moon and clouds had all disappeared. Distant treetops appeared for a moment before darkness swooped over them again. I rubbed my eyes and looked once more. The blackness had become the silhouette of a vast bat's wing blocking out the moon. With distance the black shape transformed into the shadowy appearance of an immense flying lizard. Now there were two, diminishing into darkness as they flew swiftly away above the clouds.

I ran the rest of the way back to the road past foliage frosted platinum by moonlight. "I can't stand happy endings," I muttered as I got in my car and drove away.

A Quickie

Seems like only yesterday
that it was yesterday.
Seems like just a little
while until tomorrow.
Seems like now is going by.
Now is going by
quick as the eye can follow.

Before the happiness
and after the sorrow,
who would ever guess
that in between the no and yes,
poised in the middle of birth and death,
is nothing but this single breath
that is now going by,
now going by.
Now is going by
quick as the eye can follow.

What if all history and religion
and science too,
all the poverty and riches
were nothing but a trick
that's being played on you,
a conspiracy of magicians and witches
who cast their spells
without knowing what they're doing,
who screw themselves
without seeing who they're screwing,

who swallow up each moment
without even chewing,
who don't have a clue
that the magic of
us and them and me and you
is now going by,
now going by.
Now is going by
quick as the eye can follow.

Section Five

If literature is just the fact that someone unknown is reading this now, then doggerel is literature.

Hot Allegories & Sweet Metaphors

Seeing from the beginning that she was contaminated by human confusion had not saved him from the illusion that she belonged to herself and not to them.

Tiger!

Long ago before your time there lived a primal tiger in his prime. His eyes at night reflected the light of the moon as tall strands of grass would sway with his breath. He embodied life and sometimes death. His footfalls were swift and strong, teeth sharp, claws long. At the timbre of his roar, powerful and sweet, every tigress in the jungle would go into heat.

All of nature received him and night birds sang as he silently approached a field of sugar cane, drawn by the sound of lovesick moans and the delicious scent of tigress vagina pheromones.

When she saw him slipping toward her between the trees, pale shadows of branches sliding across his thick, striped fur, she called with a small voice that sounded at once like a sneeze, a whine and a purr. She yawned and stretched with her tail twitching in the air (revealing the treasure that awaited him there). Around her neck there gleamed a chain that bound her to a tree bearing ripe plantains.

Seeing her bondage he knew right then she was part of a trap that had been set by men. He could see the banyan leaves and wild wheat woven loosely together in a flimsy mat stretched across a large pit with long, sharp-pointed wooden stakes planted upright and waiting to tear into his flesh. As he inhaled he could taste the newly dug earth and smell the freshly cut wood. He could easily see and effortlessly dodge their awkward attempt at camouflage. With a hint of arrogance in his stride, he walked to the edge of the hidden abyss and leaped across to stand at her side.

She glanced at him, looking him in the eye before turning away to lick her paw and whisper a feline sigh. He sniffed her nose and nibbled on her ear. She leaned against him and he felt a tremble pass through her skin. When he chewed gently on her neck, the chain made a small clinking sound. She lay down beside him on the ground and pressed her forepaw against his chest, waited for him to come closer. He paced back and forth looking at her face, then he did come closer as she waited and rubbed his cheek across the white fur of her belly. She whimpered a tiny yowl while her scent was telling him *I'm ready now*. He entered her in a single long slow stroke while she moved from side to side slightly and up and down. In this way they began their night-long ride on each other that ended at last with a deep growl and a final thrust into the moist heart of her grip. Then he slipped out and rolled over to lay on his back and look at the sky.

With her hind legs she suddenly delivered such a powerful kick that it sent him tumbling into the pit! At the same time that one stake pierced the flank of a leg another was passing through the flesh of his upper abdomen not far from the heart. Somehow his front claws had caught the edge of the pit and he howled in pain as he pulled his bleeding form onto solid ground again. Then as he stared at her in disbelief she raked her claws across his face and tried to reach him with her teeth.

He crawled back into the rainforest leaving a track of dark blood behind him. In deep undergrowth, he finally stopped to roll on his back and writhe in agony as he waited to die. Then his consciousness faded away.

When he awoke it was to the heat of mid-day. The blood that covered him was mostly dry. A vagrant breeze carried the fragrance of human sweat. Sounds of men's voices and of their clumsy steps followed closely behind. They were following his track! They were drawing nearer and nearer! Any forest denizen could have found his trail, but not these men. They could not smell anything that did not stink. They did not listen but only think. They were in too much of a rush to notice leaves that were crushed in the underbrush.

So he escaped to a cavern in the side of a hill and learned to survive though the power of will. He learned to leap with his injured leg, to land on his side so not to open the wound in his belly. He learned to feed on small game and when he was very hungry to gnaw on the roots of certain plants. When urges arose that led toward the sexual dance, he'd remember her face as she betrayed him and the pain of his wounds would become inflamed. Seeing from the beginning that she was contaminated by human confusion had not saved him from the illusion that she belonged to herself and not to them.

Years passed. With the leg that dragged he learned to limp and the limp was slowly incorporated into the grace of his gait. Antelope fell once more beneath the power of his claws. He began again to practice mighty roars that expressed each moment's beauty and pain.

A young tigress heard his roar as it penetrated the forest and she heard the silence that followed reverberating in the leaves of bushes and in the roots of her fur.

The Storm

"... And Out Of The Windmill Labyrinth,
An Angel Sings No Finite Song ... "

The sudden gale tore flirting sheets and fleeting shirts from the lines to which they clung and flung them to the trees.

"Jeeze!" said Molly Harris, as if she'd never seen the wind before and held her breath and pointed like a child. End over end a garbage can tumbled down the street, roaring and clanging into fire hydrants, cars and an occasional frightened cur. Dogs yelped, the wind howled, rain came, strumming, thumping and skittering across aluminum siding, concrete, leaves and your cheek.

You stood there, your hair wet and plastered against your neck and ears, water dripping off your nose as though you were the captain of a mackerel fleet stealing your living from the storm. In fact you were shooting the evening news for TV.

"Come on! We've seen enough!" I cried, but you just snorted and wouldn't even glance at me. Your eyes were on fire.

"Oh, But listen . . ." and I laid my hand on your arm.

"Enough?" you gasped. "Enough?" You blinked and whistled furiously and, in a rage I couldn't understand, hissed at me, "Don't you see? It's just begun!!!"

Your station's weather reports were inconclusive and smug, a repetition of warnings issued moments before. Astrologers were interviewed who vied for the credit of having predicted the storm while frequent news flashes were precious minutes behind and volleys of rain like machine gun fire strafed our sidewalks and homes.

On the high school lawn the marble form of Our Lady Josephine of the Strawberries, haven for the poor from Heaven's fury, teetered and fell. Her head broke off and was swept down Main Street by the wind, rolling faster and faster while the skies screamed like ten thousand Siamese cats in heat. Following behind Our Lady's head like the wake of a ship was the sudden appearance of cracks and fissures in the pavement. Large chunks and little chips of asphalt were torn loose into a whirling rubble juggernaut which now uprooted lampposts and flitted from building to building, plucking every board and brick into its soaring vortex. Residents were left on their knees and trembling beneath the grey and yellow swollen epileptic sky.

I had run home, looking for Edna and the kitten. My front door was open and the house empty. I was in the living room when the house seemed to sway, groan and, suddenly as a sneeze, was blown away. The wind struck me like an enormous wet rag. I staggered backward, gasping, and felt my shirtsleeves tatter and my garments being rent from my body by the force of the storm. I ran, naked and stumbling, accelerated by the wind, through mud and grass and over stones. At first my feet scarcely touched the ground. Then my feet did not touch the ground at all. Trees swayed like weeds of the field and nothing was familiar of what had been our village.

A swarm of starlings banked their flight against the wind and were scattered like pollen or feathers across the heartland of the mind. I cried. And was swept as I wept past the domain of the common eye.

I was lifted higher and higher, like a windswept leaf. There was no way to resist. Weeping, my hair being blown all over my head, standing with legs spread slightly apart and both feet planted firmly in mid air, nude, arms folded across my chest, I was carried above the frenzied treetops. It was there that I beheld Wanda Wonderly! Stretched out, writhing, pale and naked, ecstatic with fear, crying out words I could almost hear, Wanda was soaring past me. I caught her and held her to me and began to caress her breasts soothingly. At first she struggled like a wild and terrified creature. When her eyes finally focused in on my face, she relaxed and sighed, "Oh, Samuel! Sam! Sammy!"

Her nipples became hard in my hand; her breast filled my fingers and overflowed; she turned and wrapped her arms about my neck, her legs around my legs and put her tongue in my mouth. I felt her tears on my cheek and my own tears came in waves and our trembling bodies hung together on the wind.

Pause. . .

Wanda's husband, Jonah, was the town mortician, a big moose of a man who'd let it be known from bar to bar that "if anyone looks at my wife with eyes of lust, I'll tear off his cock and feed it to the dogs." This gives us pause. . .

But on the other hand, my fingers were exploring Wanda's thighs. I said, "Wanda, why did you marry that possessive undertaker? You, who are so afraid of dying, when death is his living and he likes to talk shop?"

"Stop," she whispered, her warm breath rushing in my ear. "Don't you want me?"

I answered without words. As I entered her, her eyes found mine. Trees wept leaves, dandelions blossomed, streams trembled against muddy riverbanks and flowed across the barren plains. And a tricycle bell chimed.

Ching! Ching! Ching!

The bell was getting louder. Rapidly approaching was a skinny, long nosed, bucktoothed, pimply faced teen age boy curled up in the fetal position and rolling like a wheel or a tumbleweed across the turbulent sky. As he reeled and pitched toward us, he was cranking away vigorously at a chrome bell strapped to his ankle. He had an immense hard on. From under his armpit he offered a red faced smile.

"Oh! It's Bobby Quigley! I don't want him to see me!" cried Wanda and buried her face in my shoulder as though that would somehow hide her nakedness.

"Who?" I inquired.

"Bobby Quigley. He follows me around and writes these beautiful love poems but never says anything. I think he's afraid to talk to me."

Bobby was suddenly alongside of us. "Hi!" he said in a voice that squeaked and broke. He pressed a neatly folded piece of paper into Wanda's hand and veered off to the right. I watched him disappear into a thick mist.

Wanda read what he had written and smiled, brushing away a tear. She handed me the note. Through ink that was beginning to run on wet paper, I read

And out of the windmill labyrinth
an angel sings no finite song.
Oh monkey heart parades its fancy,
earth and trees their sex outstretch.
And in echoes that hang beneath rainclouds
or sparkles that dazzle in the air full of sun
dwelleth ages of your being,
flee-eth signs that you have been.

"What does it mean?" I asked.

"Does it have to mean something?" she replied, giggling and applying a series of quick wriggling sidelong twitches to my slow downward thrust. We fucked.

* * *

Ancient thunders rumbled and darkness mounted us like a dog in heat. More rain came. Lightning came, tearing the empty sky apart, rising in jagged electric slashes and illumining our bodies in a shuddering fluorescent glow. The wind was a river bearing us swiftly along its racing currents. Banks of grey clouds rose and fell like startled cliffs on either side or surrounded us like flocks of pigeons to just as quickly disappear. Wanda's face tossed ecstatically from side to side in slow motion strobe light flashes. Her nails raked my back.

It was about then that Jonah appeared. Above the growls and echoes of thunder I faintly heard someone cry, "Hey! You're fucking my wife!" I looked up and there he was, rising out of a black cloud like the Loch Ness monster, lightning breaking and playing about his head. His fist was clenched and shaking. His face was clenched and shaking. His neck and arms were distorted by rage and lightning so that he looked like he was made of straining vein and sinew or wet mother of pearl. He was not twenty feet away! Wanda was pulling my hair and biting my ears. She did not see him. With her joyful whimpers in my ear and the moaning and whistling skies, I could no longer hear what he was screaming. Then, between lightning flashes, he disappeared. My heart was beating against my rib cage as though it were trying to escape. The sky was hissing, Wanda was kissing me, and it was quite a while before I felt sure he was gone.

The lightning came closer and closer together but from further and further away till there was only a continuous flickering glow, no slashes or streaks visible anymore. The thunder was a distant murmur and then became a constant Ohmmmmmmmm.

Somehow, smoothly, the black and grey sky opened up into a peaceful, pellucid, champagne colored electric plateau with reflections of lightning flickering like thousands of tiny tongues or sparkles across our bodies. We drifted lazily now while the sky hung still about us. Or we floated while breezes gently brushed against us whispering hush and fell away.

We looked into each other's eyes and felt the whole fantastic adventure through which we had flown to this moment and could only laugh. Our laughter played a duet, hers sounding like chimes and mine like a cello, each falling in and out of the other's delight.

Meanwhile, through the constant stroking of our bodies by the wind, our nerve endings had been stimulated into a state of generalized excitation. When I touched her neck, I couldn't tell where the feeling in my fingertips ended and the responses in her skin began. There were no neutral areas left on our bodies and our sensations melded together so that even our noses brushing against each other was a peak erotic experience intense as normal penetration. The juices of our fucking had spread through and permeated our bodies, saturating us in the sensuality of love. She was floating on her back and I was riding her like a velvet raft. My erect lingum slipped out of her yoni as my tongue touched a nipple and we soared on the sensations like high notes on a violin.

I ran my lips lightly down to her navel and the heat in us became even more intense. Her flesh and mine were vibrating in such close, high resonance it could have shattered crystal. My face was drawn irresistibly to the rise of her pubic arch. Even the patterns there of her reddish blond down had the appearance of a divine natural design infinitely rich in sexual meaning, a poem expressed in genetic language full of metaphors and mandalas that told of Life's essence and drive. The lips of her sweet vagina were slightly parted and her clitoris was pertly erect, raised up toward my eyes like a flower to the sun. Like flower and sun, my lips and her labia drank each other in. I kissed her thighs and ran my tongue in circles around the hot spot of her budding clit, brushing against it ever so lightly and then slid my tongue all the way into her fresh tart tasting vagina, wriggling it around inside like a dancing dervish.

Then it was as though we slipped into another dimension. Her pubic area became the sea, my tongue a flock of seagulls circling in the brilliant heat of the sun then skimming the surface with wingtips, sometimes dipping their bellies in flight or diving deep after some swimming motion perceived ravenously and let go of in ecstatic surrender. This seemed to go on forever until Wanda's body convulsed with joy and we had to stop because she was now so sensitive that the slightest touch was painful. We wrapped our arms around each other and our kisses were raindrops full of reflections falling gently into a crystalline pond.

* * *

A blast of cool damp wind shook our bodies and quickly dispersed. We looked around as though just awakening from a dream. Approaching from all directions like a swarm of fruit flies were dozens of little specks in the sky. As they came closer we saw that they were the other residents of the storm, all naked and absorbed in their own situations, some dazed, frightened or depressed, others having the time of their lives. They flew past at every possible angle, riding lazy undercurrents or drawn into playful crossdrafts, drifting back in slow ebbs and dropping again into one or another of the flows. There was a downdraft through which I watched several people cascade one after the other as though they were taking turns on a gigantic waterslide.

Bobby Quigley rolled by. His chrome bell was gone but he'd learned some new tricks, seemed to have figured out the secrets of movement through the sky. I watched him glide upside down a ways, suddenly spin and take off, jerking, wobbling and weaving in and out among the others. A white haired old lady waved gaily after him as he lurched, grinning, past a married couple who were fighting so intensely that they'd missed the whole storm. A bunch of kids tumbled by playing freeze tag. Their innocent joy and playground laughter filled the air, fading as they drifted away.

It was then that I noticed Edna and the kitten. Clouds close behind had caught a mysterious light and reflected it around her in a shimmering nimbus. She was standing in the

air with eyes lowered, her body bare, in sad and humble patience, the wet kitten suckling at her breast, a surreal madonna and child. She began to weep, glancing in our direction but quickly averting her gaze. I wondered if she'd seen me partaking of the nectar of Wanda's forbidden fruit, drunk on the impermanence of ever changing love. A warm draft licked up at us and lifted Wanda and me higher and higher. I kept watching below as distance diminished the dimensions of Edna's tableau vivant till we passed through a warm mist and found ourselves once more alone in an empty chamber of the sky. Dark clouds hovered above and below and all around the luminous clearing in which we now embraced.

Wanda slid down my body as though she were lowering herself down the trunk of a tree. With her left arm wrapped around my knees, her right hand guided my erection to her delighted licks and kisses. She gave me head! She went down on me! She licked my dick! She sucked my cock! Oh, my god, it was insanely good! As she took the head of my penis into her mouth, her features were all sensual abandonment and innocence and the most beautiful angelic face I've ever seen. My shaft was wet with her saliva and her face was wet with the rain and the rain was slow and steady and warm. Wanda increased the enthusiasm and pace with which she engaged my sexual lightning rod and I realized that she wanted me to come now!

A little trickle of liquid excitement slid tickling through my innards, closely followed by a contraction that frolicked down my spine and quickly developed into an implosion of the heart and abdomen, an ecstatic convulsion of epic proportions, a release of all the joy and terror and wonder of our adventure, such an exuberant outburst of semen that some of it slipped out of her parted lips and moistened the down on her cheek. She took me deep into her mouth, sucking blissfully for whatever might be left.

At that very moment a sudden explosion of thunder and light and wind roared at my back, propelling me into blind confusion. I felt Wanda let go of my legs and slip away. Blinking after her with dazzled eyes, I saw her disappear into a cluster of dark billowy clouds. She was gone!

As I cried after her "WANDA!!!", a huge hand clamped down on my shoulder from behind. I turned my head to see that I was in the grip of Jonah's fury. He whirled me around and his fingers dug into my shoulders, penetrating to the bone. I was helpless. A sudden chill wind howled in my ears. I looked into his pale vicious bloodshot eyes and beheld the rage of death! His voice reverberated, piercing the storm. "Are you ready, Samuel Beast?! Do you know who I am?!"

"You're the Goddam mortician," I cried. I was scarcely able to catch my breath. "You would have gotten me sooner or later anyway! You've always been waiting! You're the Angel of Death!"

"Then how dare you ignore my power?!" he roared. "And how dare you fuck with my wife?!!"

"That's Life and it was worth it," I replied. I was shaking all over, but ready to die.

He growled and hissed. "You'll never seduce anyone's wife again. You'll never even know a kiss. I'm going to destroy every trace of your physical being so that you are less substantial than dust or mist. All that will be left of you, Samuel, will be the wind. You'll whisper to all forms, always sighing because you'll have no shape of your own. You'll travel across the world with no place to rest. No one will see you. You'll be eternally alone."

He tore my body in half.

And so it is that I forever tell this story, sing this song describing the rigors of the storm; and how I came to be the wind that swoops down from the rafters, creeps up through cracks in the floor, rattles against your window panes, hisses through your lungs, explores the unknown regions of cellular caverns, swims through your blood and sweeps through your mind.

I am now the movement of space itself, embracing every object and motion, soaring beyond the fiery breath of the sun to where other stars play and spin. At the same moment I am penetrating the fibers of your clothing to brush against the textures and planes of your skin. And this is how it shall be until the end.

A Cameo Appearance by Sentience

At last we arrived at our old campsite. We found several people gathered around the fire pit, none of whom we'd ever before met. I sat down on the big log beside a skinny, extremely sensitive redheaded nymph with freckled complexion and intense green eyes. She introduced herself as Janice. Before I could reply with my own name, a fat, furry middle-aged man who'd been sitting on a rock suddenly stood and declared, "I am the Beast of Love. Since the veils of confusion have fallen from my eyes, I've been driven mad by the beauty I see. There's nothing I can do about these attacks of insanity except to share them as tales with anyone who will listen. Now look at you. . ."

He began pacing around the circle, looking into each person's eyes. He was a preposterous looking being with hair and beard that were long and white and twisted. Into his facial expressions a look sometimes would creep that said he was playing it for laughs but also that he was playing for keeps.

He said, "If you were children of the universe (which at least sometimes you are), if you were living on a planet that occupied one place at a time in infinite space, planet that revolved about a star, star that's one of such multitudes as a mist of lights filling the skies above the shore, if you lived in packs or hives or flocks or tribes or cities, if you spoke in sounds and silence and facial expressions and the meanings of grace-filled bodily movements, if all these conditions could somehow be met, then I'd tell you one of the strangest stories I've heard yet. Are you ready?"

"I'm ready!" shouted an impatient, bloated, dusty albino.

The Beast of Love began. "This is the tale of a being named Prank, also known as Sentience, who comes from a universe of no dimensions, no space or time or mass or motion."

"Come on, just tell the story," heckled the irritable, slow-witted albino.

"All right!" responded Beast enthusiastically. "One day as I was taking a warm Bath and contemplating the pure math of fractal designs expressed in snowflakes and in every living cell, in clouds and mountains and leaves on trees, in the whirling dances of Galaxies, in capillaries and nerves and DNA, in vision and music and toward and away . . ."

"Cut the bull!" yelled the abominable retarded albino.

Beast smiled at the white one and continued, "Okay. Anyhow, Prank suddenly appeared Grinning and naked alongside me in the tuB. It was oBvious at once that I was seeing an alien Being, which I took as a Bad sign concerning my mental health. To make matters worse, he immediately Began to ruB my Body in ways that were more than merely intimate."

"Hoo boy!" screamed the perverted, mentally disturbed albino.

Beast paused for a moment, then went on. "His touch penetrated my skin as he explored my sensations through muscles and organs to the very marrow of my Bones.

'Hey! Cut it out!' I cried, squirming like a schoolgirl the first time she's fondled on a date.

Prank smiled a charming smile and asked, 'Why?'

'Well, first,' I replied, 'Because you're an alien life form that most likely exists just as a figment of my mind.'

'Then what's the problem?' he asked, stroking my liver as though he were it's lover . . . or mine.

'Well, I hate to admit it,' I said, 'But when it comes to my own sexual preferences, I'm a little Bit homophoBic. And you do appear to Be a male.'

'Ahhh,' he responded. 'I'm an hermorphrodite and a shapeshifter. I can be whatever you like.' With those words, his penis shrank and inverted into a most lovely vagina. Limbs and features became more slender and delicate, heavy fur became light fine down. Breasts grew with upright nipples at the ends. 'Now,' she asked, still touching me within, 'can we be friends?'

'I don't know,' I answered, very near to tears. 'Although you look human and female and beautiful in every other way, it makes me uneasy that you still have four legs, six arms, wings and antennae.'

'This is just how I appear for you,' she said.

'Are you an hallucination?' I asked.

'No more or less than anything else you've ever experienced,' was her reply. 'My name is Prank, And you, if I'm not mistaken, call yourself Beast.'

'Sometimes I do,' I replied. 'And I'd appreciate it if you'd ask permission when you get the urge to feel me up inside.'

'Too late,' she laughed. 'I am the Prank of Sentience. And I've been the feeling of your feeling since you were conceived.'

'I'm reassured (but not relieved) if you've always been the experience of sensation,' I said, feeling for the moment like a puppet on a string. 'But are you my sentience or the awareness of existence in every living thing?'

'Both,' she laughed. 'How could it be otherwise? I am the seeing of everything with eyes. Look . . .' She turned into a leopard, then an arctic seal, then a mermaid there beside me in the tub, then once again to the strange being of many appendages and limbs. 'I am exclusively yours. Welcome to the club,' she said. transforming even as she spoke and smiling as though it were all one great joke.

All I could possibly think of to say was, 'Why have you suddenly appeared to me this way?'

'Well', she replied, 'when you pondered fractal patterns and DNA it was almost the same as if you had been calling out my name. Also, the fact that you like stories is well known all across the abyss. And I have one for you . . .'

"The tale she told went something like this . . . "

The filthy mindless idiot albino interrupted. "Hey! Is this going to be one of those stories within a story within a story?"

"Yes," sighed Beast, "and I call it. . . .

Prank's Joke

A rabbi, a porcupine and a crackhead walked into a bar. The rabbi said to the bartender, "Whiskey for us all, if you don't mind."

"Sorry," the barkeep replied, "but I make it a rule never, ever to serve your kind."

"What's that supposed to mean?" the rabbi demanded.

"My name's Maurice Frank," the bartender said, "though most folks call me Mo. I don't think of myself as a bigot, but that doesn't mean it isn't so. For example, I can look at you and see that you're an arrogant jew. You think you're one of the chosen few. You flaunt your Yawah and Moses and Jesus and Marx and Freud and Einstein too; try to make us gentiles feel as though we're not as good as you.
Your porcupine friend will stick up for you whether you're wrong or right. He lacks the intelligence for little other than a bloody fight.
Not to mention this crackhead who thinks of nothing but what he himself needs. Thievery and lies are the most noble of his deeds. You're all nothing but trouble and I'm asking you to leave."

"Wait!" cried the rabbi. "We've heard how we look to one seeing through your eyes. Now I beg you to listen to our replies."

"Go ahead," said Mo, glancing down with a skeptical frown.

"Personally, I'm no Einstein or Moses", **the rabbi said,** "but I do keep their books upon my shelves. I respect them, not for ethnic superiority, but because they cared more for humanity than for themselves. I honor their example every day by trying to be kind and generous in my own humble way."

"And I," said the porcupine, "am a peaceable, somewhat lazy fellow. My primitive pincushion features are worthless for aggression but make perfect sense as a means of self defense."

The crackhead spoke in a hoarse whisper. "I'm everything you said and worse. I've been a victim of addiction since I was an innocent kid. But I ain't innocent no more. There's not a rotten thing I haven't done. Tonight I stopped these two on the street, begged them for money, lied to them that I wanted to get something to eat. And even though they knew that being around me is risky, they offered to bring me in here and buy me some whiskey and listen to the stories that behind my face are hid so they could help me understand who I am and why I've done the things I did."

Mo Frank looked at them each and shook his head. **"You know the old saying about how it's never too late for regret … or is it never too soon? I forget. But you've touched my heart and I'm truly sorry for the things I said. You may stay and order whatever you like. In fact your first drink will be on me."** So saying, he placed three shot glasses before them and with the cheapest house whiskey, filled each glass half of the way.

The rabbi looked at his glass with a squint and a nod. "It's half empty!" **he howled.** "Is this how you treat the chosen of God?"

"He's right!" declared the porcupine, his quills stiffening into swords. "These half empty glasses are a greater insult than your words."

"If I were you, brother," the crackhead was heard to say, "I'd fill these glasses the rest of the way."

The bartender reached for his gun. The porcupine's spikes were wildly extended. The crackhead slipped his knife out of its sheath. The rabbi was about to utter a cabalistic curse. Things were looking bad and about to get a whole lot worse . . . when in walked Lila, the holy whore also known as the Goddess of Sexual Love. Her legs and the cleavage of her breasts were brazenly showing. Her lips and her tongue were made for kissing and licking.

"Before any of you bad boys makes one more move," she said in a low voice that teased as though she were telling a lover how to please her, *"make sure what you do is not because you have something to prove."*

When her words they did hear, all four males shifted gears.

The porcupine spoke with an arrogant sneer and a blink. *"I am,"* he said, *"therefore I think."*

"Sure you do," she answered, *"in your own porcupine way."*

The rabbi offered to buy her a drink, mentioning under his breath that the servings were somewhat small.

The crackhead's posture improved and he seemed almost tall as he inquired if she ever did drugs.

"Not the kind you use," she replied with a shrug.

Mo Frank winked an eye and longed to touch her skin. **"Thank you, Lila,"** he said, **"for dropping in."**

"I want to tell you a secret," **Lila said to all four.** *"And this is strictly between us. But not one of you is as aware in your mind as you are in your penis."*

After a dramatic pause, Beast went on, "And that, my friends, was Prank's joke indeed. Except that as she said the word 'penis', she mounted mine and began to ride me like a cowgirl on her favorite steed."

"Yes!" cried the disgusting, brain-dead albino.

Beast rolled his eyes and said, "I asked her again if she was an illusion, something I was making up at that very moment.

She replied, 'On the contrary, it's taken me since the beginning of time to manifest you so that you could be mine. I've grown your bones out of stones, extracted your blood out of oceans, nerves out of cobwebs, muscles and tendons out of stalks in fields and your skin from the petals of wildflowers.'"

Beast's voice had become a whisper. "I couldn't help but ask her why. And this, word-for-word was her reply,

'So that for a little while we could ride together the magic horse of being through this forever changing landscape of Now.'"

Before he sat down again, Beast looked around to see if anyone had understood.

"Your story sucks!" shouted the accursed, evil albino.

"Isn't Prank's joke a bit anti-Semitic?" asked Janice, "An insult to anyone who happens to be a Jew?"

The demonic, demented albino commented, "You demean porcupines and crackheads too!"

"No, no, no!" answered Beast. "Don't you see? It could just as well have been a Catholic priest, a wart hog and a politician. Or a Buddhist, a rhino and a dirt-for-brains albino."

"Then the story really sucks," the unkind pathetic albino whined.

A Bad Dream

So I had this dream, see? Where you wasn't you and I wasn't me. We was two other guys. But it was really us and we was ridin around in this new Chevy convertible with the top down. We just got paid and was lookin to get laid, okay?

So we seen two chicks who've got nice big boobs and tiny waists and little hips and long pointy fangs stickin out past these really pretty pouty lips. You're drivin and ya pulled right over by em and called out, "Hey girls!"

They giggle and look at each other and the redhead jabs the blonde one in the ribs. I turn to you and say, "Hey! Are you nuts? These girls ain't sluts. They're vampires!"

Well yer mind was set. I could see it in yer eyes. You said, "Don't give me no shit. Just look at those tits! Ain't you the one who's always sayin that somethin's worth doin is worth takin a risk?"

Well, I got to admit I say that a lot. Not in real life but in this dream, ya see? So ya got me on that one. And besides, the redhead is lookin me up and down like she's so hot she's gonna explode. So I tell ya, "I think we'll be okay as long as afterward we don't fall asleep."

So the next thing I know is we're in this motel and I'm playin my guitar and they're both dancin and gettin undressed. Then the redhead comes over and sits on my chest and puts her little finger in my mouth. "Bite me," she says. "I like to play rough."

"You gonna bite back?" I ask her.

She just smiles with those sharp fangs showin and says, "I guess we'll see."

So then the lights're out and it's dark and her and me are pumpin away and in the other bed I hear the blonde let out a cry like she's gettin born and you groan like it's yer last breath. Right about then I feel those damn fangs go deep inta my shoulder. Now I don't wanna die, but I'll be damned if I'm gonna show that it hurts. So I start laughin and she does too, even while she's bitin. That's when I sit up in bed and finally realize it was a dream the whole time.

"Man! That's a fucked up dream!"

Yeah.

"So did ya tell Barb?"

You kiddin? Hell no! Tell her I even dreamed about gettin it on with another woman, vampire or not, and I'd be toast.

Sea Of Breath

It was a very intense meditation: I was diving for pearls in a sea of breath, clothed only in my innocence. Seaweed tendrils wet tickling fingers stroked my flesh at a thousand points of moist sensation while I descended. Soon I traversed into depths where schools of curious, skittish brightly colored tropical fish fluttered through a playground of bony coral reef.

In the gentle flow of Now I'd regained my eyes, forgotten my "I", realized that whatever is shown and seen is precisely in a place and at a time where no one else has ever been.

An inviting blissful current drew me to a cave. Above the entrance was clearly engraved "Suspend All Beliefs and Disbeliefs, Ye Who Enter Here". Inside there was no illumination except the sensitivity of my own vision. Sea lichen were clinging to walls and rocks, every cell of their being so aroused by water's touch that they lived their entire lives as orgasming clusters of sentience. Baby crustaceans played games of mock paranoia and genuine bliss. There were countless tunnels disappearing into all directions, one of which distinguished itself to my sight by subtle patterns of shadow and reflections indicating a distant source of light. Swiftly did I swim into that tunnel, sometimes having to duck my head and shrug shoulders to squeeze through its rocky passages.

The labyrinth rotated at sharp angles like elbows and knees. I navigated a section of narrow dimensions through which I scarcely could fit. Around a corner there appeared the glow of a far off area that was mysteriously lit. I swam straight toward it.

Through the maze's twists and turns I went. I was like an infant passing through the birth canal on its way to being born. Eventually I entered a larger cavern that was bathed in the same gentle radiance as a morning sky the moment before dawn. Swimming toward me were half a dozen tiny seahorses with iridescent blue transparent skin. No larger than my fingers, they drifted and hovered in place, gazing at me with round blue eyes that occupied most of their faces. One of them zipped up to my lip and took a nip, a sharp pinch followed by more as the others tasted my cheek, neck, arms and a nipple. While they were biting me again and again, I looked up and saw a swarm of thousands of seahorses more, each rushing to take a needle quick prick of my skin. As they drew near I could see in their dance the numberless variations of painful circumstance. Their scalpel-sharp small teeth did not hurt so much as sting, each bite leaving behind a little trickle of blood. I was covered in seahorses from the bottoms of my feet to the top of my head! All through their furious attack I kept swimming on. I wanted to turn back to a darker area where I imagined they'd leave me alone. But I was drawn like a moth toward the secret of the light.

Still performing as host to countless voracious little lips, I swam out of frazzled anguish into a chamber so enormous and bright that it dazzled my eyes. From this grotto there was a large opening leading to the open sea. The light came from out there, spilling into shadows cast by a sizzling brilliant phosphorescent display, radiating from a source that could not be seen from within the cave.

With one final nip of an eyelid, abruptly all the seahorses swam away from me toward the hole that led to that light. There they converged before my astonished eyes into one great shimmering seahorse more than three times my size! Each of the little ones had become a scale or a cell upon its mother!

It was too much to be seeing! I glanced down for an instant and noticed that because of how much I'd bled, my entire body looked as though I'd been painted red. Was I swimming or leaping or dancing? I could not tell! The giant seahorse stared at me and trumpeted a loud high-pitched squeal.

I feared this shrill alarming sound was an expression of delight at encountering her next meal. I dove and slithered into a small space between some rocks and a wall, where hopefully she could not reach. I couldn't hide but only watch with my eyes open wide as she approached.

She towered above my shelter, reared back and snorted then sneezed an eruption of bubbles out of her nostrils. She swayed from side to side in a state of high agitation. Then she opened her mouth. . . and spoke.

"My name is Meriad," she said, a slight tremor passing like a wave across the finny mane at the top of her head. "I am Guardian of the Light." She almost disappeared in a sudden throbbing burst of brightness. Then she went on to say, "You certainly are a fool to be so stubborn and brave as to face me here in my own cave. I could tear you to pieces before you could twitch one eye. But for some reason or another, I am reluctant to see you die."

She propelled herself backward with a whir of fins that moved like fantastic transparent blue wings. "One of the things I may do," she said with a languid blink, "is to assume any form of which you might think. From various stations in each role you give me, I will let you see why you must go while you still live."

Her scales wriggled a little then danced like a field of grass in a storm. As one removing a costume and mask, she stripped off her seahorseness and transformed into my mother . . . who wore her blue flannel robe, hair up in curlers with cold cream upon her slightly blue cheeks.

"Oh, my God!" my mother cried. "What do you think you're doing? You're going to drown! You can't breathe under water! You can't inhale through the pores of your skin!"

"But, mother, I am!" I couldn't help but reply.

Her face convulsed into weeping and while she bitterly cried, my mother turned her head aside. She glanced back at me over her shoulder and I found myself looking into Meriad's eye. The seahorse yawned and unfurled a long hummingbird tongue. She shook all over till her scales vibrated like sequins or feathers. When her movements subsided she had entered into the person of my father.

He was wearing his blue pinstripe suit, thumbs in the pockets, corners of his mouth turned down in that infamous pout. "Look at what you've done! You've made your mother cry! If you don't leave now, she's convinced you will die."

"But, father, I'm determined to see the source of light."

He clenched his fists and winced his eyes. Blood rushed to his face, expressing the familiar rage through which he inspired fear of physical violence. "When I speak," he demanded, "you *will* observe the rule of silence! You are so selfish and naïve. I find it hard to believe that you're a son of mine. I've tried to teach you how to obtain wealth and honor among men. Be practical! Forget this adventure! Go out and grab whatever possessions and security you can. And think of your mother. You are the reason for her life."

"But she died when I was a child."

His eyes filled with grief then closed as he sadly replied, "Yes. I know. And not long after, so did I. Seeing us this way is like visiting with ghosts. Now I beg you to leave this cave and return to somewhere you'll be safe."

So saying, he dissolved into a slow motion implosion of rioting colors out of which emerged the face and form of my high school science teacher. Long ago, with his sarcastic grin and cold blue eyes, he'd seemed the most worldly wise person I'd ever met. "Now you've got yourself in a mess, don't you?" He smiled rhetorically. "I suppose you think you'll discover something new. But it's historically true that everything's the same now as it's ever been. Only science can reveal what's ultimately real. To learn science, you must memorize the words of other men, men who lived long ago and each of them was far greater than you."

"I don't want to be great!" I cried. "I just must follow my fascination with the mystery of the light."

"You're on a fool's errand then," he replied. "And it's one you might not survive."

He faded into some other dimension as another form rose out of swirls and tides and particles to take my breath away. It was Jessica, naked and ready to play. Jessica lying naked on her parents' blue couch. Lying naked first with one finger inside her yoni, then smearing her body's moisture on the pink tips of her jiggling small breasts. "If you want to touch me some day," she said, "then we'll have to be married. You have to buy me a house and my own car and pretty things for our bedroom and a beautiful yard."

"We were fifteen," I answered, "when you told me this before. Then you went with someone else who could buy you so much more. Now you're old as me and your greatest adventures are soap operas, like the ones you watch on TV. Who knows where it might have gone if your happily-ever-afters had not been inscribed in stone."

She lowered her eyes modestly and said, "You'd better get out of here. No woman will have you once you're dead." With those words she shimmered and morphed into the magical seahorse again.

Meriad looked at me out of deep contemplation then asked, "Are you ready to go?"

Without hesitation I answered, "No!"

She inquired, "Have you been so unmoved then by these threats and temptations?"

"Very moved," I responded, "but I haven't come this far on a frivolous whim."

"So I see," she sighed, those tremendous blue eyes so wild and shy. She drifted toward me through the ocean of water and breath and light. Her dragon snout quivered, nostrils flared. Her voice now gentle, she said, "Hold onto my neck and I'll take you there."

Her tail was twitching in a warm current that enveloped us for a moment before dispersing. Her beauty excited me so deeply that I felt as though my heart were bursting. Through her transparent blue skin I saw not organs and bones, but torrents of energy flowing.

I stroked her neck with my hand. She was pure sensation shivering beneath my touch. I put my arms around her neck while her tongue flicked out and licked my cheek. We floated together toward the glowing opening to her cave. Her movements became playful while I earnestly hung onto her slender neck and, out of tenderness, sang a joyful *aum* for her to hear. She wore me like a scarf or an intimate garment, my dangling legs brushing across her throat and her chest in an involuntary tactile torment of bliss.

As we passed through her chamber and into seas of intense luminosity, she lowered her head to my ear. The sound of her words was at first like a breeze, but quickly grew into a feminine choir with thousands of aged hags, ovulating women and little girls calling out, "We are now approaching the Mother of Pearls."

The lightbursts into which we moved were so powerful they blew away every thought that had ever entered my brain. I felt as though we were sailing into the winds of a hurricane. The seahorse throat to which I clung trembled and shook as she let out one mighty roar in which I could hear every song that had ever been sung.

The Mother of Pearls' brightness would have burnt out my sight but I held one hand over my eyes. Through the mask of muscles and fingers and blood and bone, I beheld the most beautiful, sacred, terrifying being I have ever known. In shifting patterns of light I see ever-changing features of human faces, such as the old masters attempted to paint. Her windblown radiant hair is flowing in every direction, atoms of each strand made up of galaxies, every flash of a quark the living feeling, hearing and seeing of another passing being. Strobing pandemonium of birth and death and day and night. Birds of light in mercurial flight. She is the feeling within all feelings, the meaning of meaning. Each precious fleeting moment she savors forever. Universes are born and die in the blink of her eye.

She moons me through a telescope, undresses under extreme magnification into networks of nerves and capillaries, textures of cellular tissues, subtlest nuances of the intimacy of perceiving, each particular of the content of experiencing, context of consciousness, mirror dissolving the boundaries between the see-er and the scene. And ever entering her from behind in furious passion is the formless one of whom we never shall speak.

Meriad plunged with me into the heart of that explosion of light. We were streaking through canyons that ran between towering jeweled castles of flame. Storms of sparks or meteors flashed past us. Then a riptide of brightness tore Meriad apart into countless tiny seahorses that fluttered swiftly out of sight. Streams of fragmented images were cascading out of springs erupting from the source of awakening and dreams.

In his final instant, a dying man is lying on his side. He experiences:

sunset over a city with evening breezes whispering *hush*   young virgin turning away to conceal a sexual blush   lovers disappearing into each other's touch   ancient redwood, roots sipping sweet California rain   high priestess perhaps holy perhaps insane, rolling her eyes in ecstasy and pain   blue flower radiating into blossom   newborns nursing in the pouch of a mother possum   crack baby abandoned in a drawer while mama goes out to get more and then more   lonely saxophone intoning a blues solo   twins in the torment of their first separation   eighteen wheel truck hurtling down the highway of night   blind man somehow miraculously regaining his sight   waterfall taste of ice cream   first kiss   last breath   . . .

Then I open my eyes. . . and you are here.

Fool's Errand

The angry tug-of-war between the Prince of Form
and the Princess of Grace has attracted a Fool,
a jester named Chester with a white painted face.
He's volunteered to dance on the tight wire
between them.

With a tip of his top hat and a tap of his toes,
with his long arms, short legs and belly that's fat,
Chester balances and prances in the very middle
of that embattled no man's land.
This Fool can trace his bloodlines through generations
of circus dwarves, momentary acrobats
and singing, rhyming not-so-silent mimes.
He raises his eyebrows, licks his lips, opens his mouth
and speaks:

"Your Royal Highnesses.
After adding all the plusses
and subtracting the minuses,
in the final analysis
I am larger than an ant
and smaller than rhinoceroses.
My life span is no greater
than a single long sigh.
But while I endure,
of this I am sure:
that you are
the taste and language
of my tongue,
the inner sanctum of my eye.
I'm a walk-on performer

with a few lines to say
and then I must die."

He nods his head
so that the hat tumbles off
and rolls down his arm
to land in his hand.
Headpiece now clasped over his heart,
he drops to one knee
and continues his plea.

"But you. . .
you are the Lovers.
You can perform
the Kama Sutra forever
or pull away from each other
till it seems that long."

Form is wearing a neatly tailored three-piece suit.
He shakes his head, puts a scowl on his face
and points his finger straight at Grace,
who's naked except for her shoes.
"She's a little girl riding around in my limousines.
She uses the technology I invent, but hasn't any clues
about why it works or what it means.
She's inconsistent and vague and always changes her mind.
If I didn't stop her, she'd stare at the sun until she went blind."

Grace gazes, with one eyebrow raised
and a look of scorn, right back into
the face of Form.
"He's a clumsy oaf in a constant state of distraction.
He gives and he takes with the intent of gain,
thinks of nothing but his own satisfaction.
He's oblivious to nuance, doesn't hear the music
that's playing behind the scenes. He has a million words
and throws them around without truly knowing

what even one of them means."

She stamps her foot and says with a pout,
"See if you can find out from that muscle-bound heel
why he never asks me how I feel."

Form turns his back and says over his shoulder,
"When one's tastes are so objective as mine,
questions about sentience are a waste of time.

"But," Chester implores,
waving one hand toward Grace
and with the other
pulling up his drawers,
"how she feels
is such a great part
of her appeal!"

"Ach!" retorts Form with a grimace and a sneer.
"All right. Is this what you want to hear?
How does she feel? The answer is plain.
Tiny electro-chemical impulses pass from
nerve cells through synapses and thus
relay a message to her divine brain:
This is pleasure! or *This is pain!*"

Grace giggles and leaps like a ballerina
across the space between her and Form.
As she falls into his arms, Form kneels
and lowers her body in repose almost to the ground.
He reaches toward her breasts
with his fingers outstretched.
She slips away in a single bound
and runs on her toes back to where she began.

"See!" cries Form. "Do you want to know why
I don't know how she feels?

It's because she's such a tease!
She throws herself into my arms
but when I try to touch her, she disappears!"

Grace puts her fingers in her ears
so she won't have to hear.
She screams, "Bastard! Asshole!"

Form is outraged.
"You bitch!" he shouts. "YOU BITCH!!!"

Their voices reverberate and echo
as the voices of deities do
when they're angry or displeased.

The Fool covers his ears
and falls to his knees.
 "No!" he howls like an injured pup.
"No disrespect meant,
but kindly shut the fuck up!"

Grace turns her shoulder and her cheek away
in a gesture of indignation.
Form clenches his fists and snarls a growl
of anger and frustration.
The jester has been rejected
and the Eternals annoyed.
He kneels, solitary and dejected,
in a glaring spotlight within
the unknowable void.
"I never should have gone for this gig,"
he mutters and sobs.
"Seemed like a good thing
while I was between jobs.
Never would have dreamed
that instead of a hero,
I'd be reduced to zero

and end up reviled
by goddesses and gods."

Still looking away from Chester, Grace complains,
"First you arrange to have us fight.
And when we do. . . "

"What?" interrupts the Fool with a shout,
"Arrange to have you fight?
 I've no idea what you're talking about."

"Yes," Grace continues. "You arranged it.
And then you think you have the right
to be so rude.
It almost makes me wish that
you couldn't see me nude."
She conceals part of her breasts
beneath her right arm
and with her left hand,
covers her pubis.
She fades into the transparency
of fine crystal glass,
so near to invisible
that Chester can scarcely see her.
She plops down on a stool
with a look of indifference on her face
and ignores both Form and the Fool.
She stretches her arms languidly
into space and sits there perfectly still.

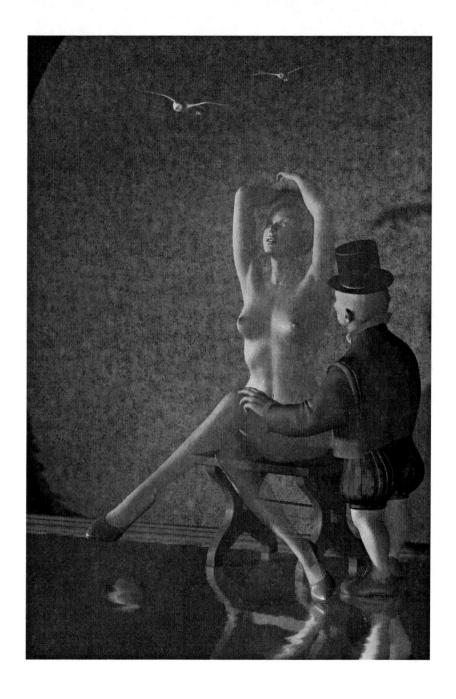

"Now you've done it!" Form declares to Chester.
"I hope you're happy. You've really impressed her."

With his mouth turned down
and tears on his face,
the Fool cries,
"Oh, no! It's over!
Look what I've done!
I've broken with Form!
Fallen from Grace!
Stumbled on the dance floor!
Tripped over my tongue!
Failed in my quest
before it's begun!"

Grace glances sideways and flutters her lashes at him
while releasing a sigh of profound compassion.

"Poor, poor mortal Fool," she whispers.
"What a mess you've got yourself in while
your life is so swiftly passing."

The spotlight that has captured Chester
in this engagement
becomes a little dimmer, softens and shimmers
as though it were the full moon reflected
on wet pavement.
Grace turns her face toward the jester
(a single teardrop on her cheek revealing).
Her voice swells with feeling,
"You're like a small child watching Mommy and Daddy fight,
begging for attention,
hoping that somehow you can make things right."

"It's true. I'm that too,"
shrugs the Fool
and shuffles his feet

then straightens his shoulders
and stands suddenly tall.
"But that's not all.
I'm also a man
who converses with
Grace and Form,
who doesn't take sides
and though he's terrified
would never hide
from the immensity
of this task."

"Why? May I ask?"
Form inquires with a sneer curling his upper lip.

"Because you were
made for each other!"
Chester cries,
giving his hat a flip,
closing his eyes,
and bobbing his head
beneath the skies
till the headpiece lands
with perfect aplomb
exactly where it does belong.

Form laughs, claps his hands and says,
"You *are* an amusing fellow.
But we have issues you can't understand, it seems.
Your attention span is limited by the extremes
of your survival deficit disorder."

The Fool wriggles his butt
and demands, "Like what?"

Form looks into the jester's eyes and replies,

"Because you are a human, Fool,
you perceive on a scale so miniscule
that a pale dwarf star exploding into a supernova
is a non-event to you."

Folding his arms in front of his chest,
Chester assumes a stance
of defensiveness and replies,
"I get your point, but
fail to see its relevance."

Grace responds, her voice gentle and kind.
"What seems to you like astrophysics or an abstraction
is a small but meaningful part of our interaction.
In the context of eternity, the swelling and bursting of that sun
passes for us like a gasp or a spark.
Imagine human lovers walking in a park
and feeling a warm breeze on their cheeks.
It's an event of which neither speaks.
But for each it's part of the ambience."

Form turns to Grace, nods his head
and murmurs, "Well said."

"We mortals experience eternity too. . ."
cries the Fool with an earnest face
that quickly melts into a silly smile.
". . . though only for a very short while."
Form gives Chester a surprised stare.
"I see," he says, "that you're not *totally* unaware."

"And though one by one we die,"
Chester adds with a sigh,
"for hundreds of thousands of years
the human race sees and touches
and thinks and hears."
He bows to Form

and Form returns the gesture
with an attitude of newfound respect.

Form says, "Beneath your silliness,
wisdom's secret is so well kept."

Chester replies
with a smile he can't help,
"Often I even keep
the secret from myself."

As the harsh spot
in which the Fool has been standing
diffuses and is expanding
into a flood of radiance
not so bright,
Grace curtseys and says,
"This puts our conversation
in a whole new light.
But I still don't understand
why you came here and made us fight."

"That's not right!"
the Fool cries.
"I don't deserve the blame.
It was *because* you were fighting
that I came."

"Ah," Form sighs. "That itself is the reason.
When you come to our plane, it's all street theatre,
pure improvisation. It's how you pay your dues.
We use what you give us so we can give you
what you use."

The Jester looks confused.
"I don't get it," he does say.

Grace interjects, "Then let me put it another way.
It's a pretty sure bet that what you look for is what you'll see
and what you see is what you get."

"Tell me," Form inquires, "what inspired you
to such a height of confusion
as to manufacture the illusion
that Form and Grace would disagree?
Surely you must be aware
of the countless perfections she and I share."

"Well," says the Fool,
"You know what they say
about an idle mind."

Grace slips into the conversation with,
"An idle mind is the devil's workshop
only when you're angry or greedy or paranoid.
Otherwise it's a playground for angels."

"Then I guess," the Fool replies,
"that I was hypnotized
by the separation of
matter and spirit
as they are seen
through my society's eyes."

Grace whispers in Chester's ear,
"Civilizations arise and disappear
in a heartbeat of the everlasting.
The culture in which you've been immersed
has only been around a few thousand years
and already it's begun to come undone."

"That's small comfort to me now,"
the Fool cries in despair.
"Let me tell you what's going on there:

Prosperity without love
devolves into greed.
Science without spiritual devotion
fills the sky with smoke
and pollutes the ocean.
Medicine that treats only
the physical as real
bankrupts the patient
before she can heal.
Religions that deny
the beauty of the senses
and proclaim a moral code
unforgiving
substitute shame and blame
for the joy of living.
I could go on and on.
There's so much more.
I won't even mention politics and war."

"Even so," Form responds, "you must have known
that Form and Grace are also Gravity and Light,
What-Is-Seen and Sight, Truth and Understanding,
a flock of birds and their flight.
It takes a great fool to think we're engaged in a fight
and even greater to believe
he could somehow set things right."

"I do my best," Chester replies.

"Yes, you certainly do," Grace responds,
blowing the Jester a kiss.
"And it's because of this
that we've decided to grant you
a cosmic favor."

Chester's mouth falls open
and his eyes become more spherical.

"You mean like a miracle?"
he asks.

"Sort of. In a way." Form does say.
"Stop me if you've heard this one before.
If you want to restore peace on Earth,
you'll have to find us a Just One first."

"Just one what?" Chester demands.

Form shrugs his shoulders and stands where he stands.
"Just one Just One," he replies.

Chester sighs.
"Just one, just one what?
I really need to know."

Form frowns and the corners of his mouth turn down.
He snaps, "Just one who is just!"

"Just one who is just. . . one?"
the Fool asks.

Grace mercifully intercedes.
"What Form is telling you that we need
is one person of your kind
who comes from the heart
as well as the mind.
One who does not submit to threats
and can't be bribed.
One who is not indentured to time
and doesn't serve greed.
One who has realized
that turning the other cheek
is not being weak.
One with the strength to be free
rather than becoming polarized.

One who, instead of reacting,
knows how to relate.
One whose personal agenda begins
with caring about humanity's fate.
One who never judges others.
A person you can trust.
A person who is just."

"Oh, yeah! I get it!" cries Chester.
"Sort of like that old thing of
*'Know yourself
and to yourself be true.'*
So if I find a Just One,
what will you do?"

A tiny smile crosses Form's face.
"Because of that person and you,"
he states, "the world will instantly become
a better place."

"Just one Just One?" Chester asks.

"That's right," Grace and Form agree. "Any one will do."

"Then anyone could be a Just One?" Chester inquires and screws up his face.

"Anyone who wills it," answers Grace.

The Fool looks over his shoulder
with a gaze so brazen
he couldn't be any bolder.
He does the one thing he can do:
He smiles and winks
directly at. . . who?

(tight close-up of the Fool winking)

Fini

Finders Keepers

Chapter 1 **Losers**

Bored, I fall over the edge of indifference. I fall into a ditch where the only options are those meanings hidden behind words. A world of mud and shit and mosquitoes big as hummingbirds. Did I mention intermittent moments of terror and disgust?

I sit at the conference table with several others in tasteful, expensive suits. Ray Resnick, a being barely evolved above a raging redneck, completes his presentation. While he's talking, I perceive what a dangerous son of a bitch he is. I decide I'd rather have him on my side than against me. So into the silence that follows, I interject, "I think Ray's hit the nail on the head. Even if his plan doesn't work, it'd be worth the budget and staff he's proposed just to learn more about the problem."

Ray flashes me a grateful smile and the deal is done. Someday he'll be a handy ally to have on my team. Bitterly, I wish I could care. *"Another 'friend',"* I tell myself, *"who will slit my throat and steal my wallet if he can. Oh my, I'm so happy."*

Nearly all of my power is drawn from the appearance of power. No one knows better than I that every significant decision in StatusQuo International is made by old man Kotropoulis himself. Kottie spends his days speculating how many pins can be stuck in the head of an angel. For sure, I'm no angel. But you know what I mean.

Kottie's indifference to the actual issues in any interaction is legendary. What matters to him is that everyone dances to his tune.

About ten years ago, I realized for certain that no one but me ever read my Monthly Reports. Instead of formal analyses framed in accounting structures, I began writing in the style of a personal journal, exposing every ugly turn of the conspiracies, coups, character assassinations and other corporate politics in which I was immersed. Of course, that was when I found out Kottie was reading the reports after all.

He sent me a note that read:

Re: April Monthly Report
What have you learned from all this?
     K.

I replied, "To function in a state of chronic depression and acute despair."

His next message simply said:

Good. That means you're becoming a realist. Be in my office next Tuesday at 7 a.m.
     K.

So I flew to the Cayman Islands, rented a car and, at 6:45 Tuesday morning, rang the buzzer at the main gate to his estate. I received directions to the front entrance of the mansion.

The door was answered by a superstar model. She wore a knit bikini with one side of the top fallen down to reveal a very pink and pert goosebumped nipple.

"You're the seven o'clock?" she asked.

I nodded. She beckoned with her finger, turned and briskly walked away. I followed her through a dozen large, densely carpeted rooms. Paintings by old masters hung on the walls. The furnishings of each room were in a different tradition. One chamber featured a small raised platform with three somber, nicely dressed musicians playing a piano, a harp and a cello. It was a beautiful, haunting sad melody that followed us for a while as we passed into other areas. At last we stopped before an oak pair of double doors. She tapped with her knuckles and turned the knob.

Kottie was sitting on the other side of an immense ebony desk. Black velvet drapes and windows were open. A warm morning breeze accompanied us into his office. Kottie stood and acknowledged me with a small bow and smaller smile. "Christie," he said, and her eyes darted quickly to his face. He pointed at his own left tit. She glanced down and, nonchalantly as someone fastening a button that had come undone, tucked away that happy teat to where it couldn't be seen. She gave me a tiny half-smile as she walked out the door.

Kottie's eyes and mine met. What a face he's got! Thinning hair. Large hooked nose. Bright eyes. A vicious look, like a bald eagle scanning the ground for prey. Or like my high school football coach when he'd get worked up before a big game. I didn't know then that Kottie maintains that attitude at all times. It's just him. He blinked across the enormous black desk at me and said, "The strong take and the weak try to survive. That's how it's always been. So you might as well be strong. Right? Take what you can get."

"I wish it were otherwise," I replied.

"If wishes were yardsticks, then fuckin' beggars would rule."

"I suppose you're right," I said.

"Of course I'm right." he said. "Let's get down to business. You're here so I can offer you a promotion."

"All right," I responded.

"Triple your salary. Stock options. Big budget. Big staff. More fuckin' perks than pigshit. But there *is* a catch. It's a test of how strong you are. The position is Vice President of Operations."

"That's Hank Barnes."

"Right."

"He's. . . "

"I know. The only real friend you've got in StatusQuo International"

"Yes. And also the best man on the entire management team."

"He's weak as pigshit; tries to be a nice guy."

"He *is* a nice guy."

"So much the worse. You're either with the program or you're out. Being nice guys is not what StatusQuo International is all about."

"What happens if I accept?"

"He's out."

"And if I decline?"

"You both keep your present positions. You won't be offered a promotion again till fuckin' you-know-what freezes over."

I chewed on that a while and finally said, "I accept."

"Good. Tomorrow I want you to tell Hank to pack up and leave. Tell him what you've done."

"That's harsh."

"Just tell him losers weepers, finders keepers. Or whatever you feel like saying. But telling him is part of the deal."

"All right."

"Good. Have a nice fuckin' day." He rotated in his chair and disappeared behind its high leather back. It seemed as though I was alone in his study. I got up and left.

Wednesday I told Hank. "I've sold out to Kottie. He gave me your job. Part of the deal is that I have to tell you to get out. Take any personal belongings with you before the end of the day. As of tomorrow, Security won't let you in the building."

"Okay," he said, and after a moment's pause with eyes averted, *"Now I'd appreciate it if you'd leave me alone."*

"Certainly," I replied, slamming the door behind me.

All that happened ten years ago. Since then I've been out to see Kottie half a dozen times more. He's in his seventies now. He'd look twenty years younger than that if not for the age spots on his forehead and hands. We've gotten to be sort of pals, to the extent that's possible in such an unequal relationship. We've played golf on his private course. Had long conversations while walking on his private beach. That was where he told me that multi-billion dollar StatusQuo International was one of his lesser holdings.

"Defense contracts. That's where I put my money for the greatest return. That's where you get to play real fuckin' hardball. What's the worst that ever happens to anyone in office politics? Someone gets fired or even goes to jail, right? In the military industrial game, assassination is little more than a playful slap. Piss us off and we'll bomb your fuckin' cities, rape your women, roast your babies, starve your parents in a refugee camp. Do you have any idea how much profit there is in one load of bombs on one plane? That's real money! That's real power! Am I right?"

"You're fuckin' right." I replied.

He regarded me with a mentor's benign smile.

I added, "But the defense contractors aren't actually the ones who start the wars."

The look on his face faded from approval to disappointment. "You're incredibly naïve," he said and walked away so quickly I couldn't catch up.

Here's a mystery I wish someone could explain to me: Kottie is impervious to flattery or any of the ploys to which those who wield great power are accustomed. But one evening as we were walking to his car, I heard the chauffer whisper, "Tonight you look marvelous, Mr. Kotropoulis." As I watched, Kottie stood a little taller and his step picked up a jaunty spring.

I get these terrible headaches that go on for days. The doctor tells me they're from stress, offered me a prescription for tranques. I told him no, thanks. I've got to keep on my toes. But wherever I go, the stress also goes. Even now, I'm driving home in my Hummer. Just forced one of those VW bugs onto the shoulder of the road. Probably the only thing that's made me smile today. No satisfaction though. Just fatigue. And the sense that though I'm no hero, I'll be standing at Ground Zero when everything blows apart.

Chapter2 **Weepers**

After my daily routine in the pressure-cooked, macabre circus of StatusQuo International, you'd think I'd get some relief when I'm with my wife and kids. I used to, I guess But lately if my family were part of a conspiracy to irritate me further, they couldn't do a better job.

Just sat down at the dinner table. Had to call the kids three or four times before they came. They ran squealing and screaming into the dining room. Now they're kicking one another under the table and giggling. Sondra giggles too, letting them know that Mommy thinks their behavior's okay. This is over the top! I can't take any more!

"All right! That's enough!" I scream. "Up to your room! Get in your jamas and turn off the light! Go!"

Tommy gives me his brattish pout and protests, "We were only playing foot tag."

I make sure he feels the power of my fury. I yell in his face, "Not one more word! Not to me or your mother or each other! Straight to bed! All of you! Right now!"

As the little one is running up the stairs, she whines, "But I'm hungry."

Sondra knows better than to ever bitch at me. But she gives me this incredulous, angry look full of. . . what is that? Confusion? That look is worse than being whipped with a thousand words.

Silently, I walk out to the patio. It's dark already. Half moon's out, stars everywhere. Not a cloud in sight. I plop down into the comfortable chair. Is it the humidity or anxiety that makes me sweat like this? It's too warm. Definitely too warm.

Sondra's starting to get fat. The kids have turned into uncontrollable brats. Nothing gives me pleasure any more. Nothing at all. Is this all there is? It's hardly worth it to be alive. Nothing seems possible except more of the same. There's no. . . Hey! There goes a shooting star. Haven't seen one of those for a while. Now it'll fade. Fade. It's not fading. It's getting brighter. Must be space debris burning as it enters the atmosphere. Any second it will disappear. It's getting bigger. Goddam! It's falling this way!! Yow!!! There it goes!!!! Right into the empty lot next door!!!!! Holy shit!!!!!! It's glowing bright as phosphorous!!!!!!! What could it possibly be? Wonder if it's starting a fire!!!! I better go see!

Chapter 3 **Finders**

That maintenance guy hasn't been out here for a while. Some of these weeds are up to my knees. There it is!!! Damn, it's bright! Hurts my eyes. Okay. Squinting helps. Don't feel any heat from it yet. Maybe al little closer. Still not hot. Damn! I'm standing almost on top of it. It's about the size of a grapefruit. What is it? A rock? A piece of metal? I can't tell because the light's too intense. When I hold my hand out, I seem to see through to the shadows of bones. No. That's got to be an optical illusion. I move my hand closer. It's not hot at all, not even warm. I could probably touch it. I do! Reality crumbles and shifts.

The vacant lot disappears without a trace. Suddenly I'm standing on the shore inside a sphere of purple sky with turquoise clouds drifting by. Large honey-colored waves rush almost to my feet. Across the sea, on the horizon, there's a flaming ball of light that possesses the features of Kottie's face. Shadows and flames wax and wane in and out facial expressions both familiar and strange. Kottie with a bright radiant halo. Saint Kottie barely containing his rage. Demon Kottie, wearing a smile of self-satisfaction. Irrational Kottie, grinning in evil idiot delight.

"Kottie!" I scream. "What's going on? What are you doing? What's this all about?"

The pounding tide replies with a roar that sounds exactly like Kottie's voice. "I'm not Kottie, you fuckin' moron!"

"I know you when I see you and it's definitely you. How did you do this? What's the point?"

"You're wrong as pigshit!" the Sun and waves answer. "Some see me as Jesus, Buddha or Mephistopheles. You see me as Kottie. In your eyes I become whatever you most believe. It's no big deal."

"Oh, yeah?" I respond. "If you're not Kottie, then who do you claim to really be?"

"Moi?" the Sun raises its shadowy brow. "I am chaos masquerading as nature. I'm perfect order disguised as happenstance. The moon is my anus. The stars are my splooge. Appearing to you is just something I do."

180

"You still look and talk just like Kottie."

"That's not my fuckin doing," he replies, then roars, "It's you!"

"Well, I want to leave," I say. "How do I get out of here?"

"That's easy," he says and for a moment flares so brightly I have to shut my eyes. "Just think of leaving and nod your head. It'll be like waking from a dream. But before you go, there's something you should know. I've traveled halfway across the universe to grant you one wish."

That stops me in my tracks. "Why me?" I ask.

"It's totally fucking random, like you won the lottery. It's predestination, the inevitable fate that's been waiting for you all along. Pardon my sarcasm, but the question is wrong. Irrelevant as pigshit. No possible answer. Are you going to make a wish or not?"

"Wait! Wait!" I interject. "Let me guess. All you want in return for this wish is my soul."

The Kottiesque Sun and the waves laugh in derision. "Your soul? Come on. If a soul *could* be sold, you'd have made the decision to cash yours in long ago. In fact, you've ignored your soul so completely that all you know about it is by hearsay. That's a good one! Your fuckin' soul! Look. If you want a wish, it's yours for free. Otherwise I've got other places to do and things to be."

"Hold on!" I cry. "If there's one thing I've learned from the internet, it's that **'FREE!'** means you'd better check the terms and conditions before you agree."

"Ain't no terms," he sneers. "And so far as conditions, there are only two. One, don't ask for the impossible. And two, don't get me mad."

"Can I wish for many wishes?" I ask.

"Try a trick like that and you'll feel my wrath." the Sun replies.

"And what do you mean *'impossible'*?"

"Once there was a woman who wished for diamond skin with copper hair, long iron claws and to stand ninety feet high. Don't ask me why. But a creature made of such materials and that tall could never have evolved on her world. So it was impossible. Instead of her wish, she got nothing at all."

"I'm beginning to see," I say. "You're a little like a genie in a bottle."

"There was one fellow who thought so, just a couple of decades ago on this very planet." the Sun responds with a snarl. "He called me Genie or Jeannie or sometimes Barbara Eden. I gather he saw me as a beautiful naked woman. His wish was for me to be his sex slave forever. Forever! Like for the rest of fuckin' eternity I was supposed to be his bitch. I threw him into a black hole where he imploded in his lust. I felt bad about it afterward. But he pissed me off."

"Hey! You're really *not* Kottie!" I yell.

For just a moment, Kotties face fades into that of a flaming cherub with fat cheeks, pouting lips and immense sad eyes. "Well, duh," he says. "How could you tell?"

"Kottie would never feel regret about anyone he's destroyed," I reply.

"It's like I told you," the Sun answers with a sigh. "I appear to you as whoever you think is most powerful. This Kottie must be quite a guy."

I nod. "He's one of the big players behind the scenes."

The Sun's nimbus sways like long golden tresses in a breeze. "What's the life expectancy for humans?"

"Up to maybe a hundred years."

The Sun blinks his eyes once and says, "Then his entire existence is hardly a blip on the constant radar. He's no bigger player than any other human. In fact, what time he does have is diminished by shutting out anything that doesn't feed his greed for domination. No, I can assure you, he's not a big player at all."

I'm a little astonished. "Kottie's not major?"

The Sun shakes his head no. His voice is matter-of-fact. "This Kottie's actually very unfortunate. He thinks his short life is about making money and controlling others. He's good at it. But what a sorry waste of the human spirit. It's a self-inflicted curse."

"I don't know what you mean."

"Didn't he tell you that a plentitude of meaningless rewards could be yours for obsessing on personal economics? That the suffering of humanity would be inflicted on you if you dared to care?"

"Oh, yeah. He said that the strong take and the weak do what they can to survive."

"Not exactly a great thought. Certainly not a world you'd want to spend your brief lifespan creating."

I'm blushing and doing my best not to give in to tears. "There's nothing I can say to that," I say.

"Nothing needs be said. Except that it's time for your wish. What have you decided?"

"I can't decide. I'm disoriented, confused. Am I hallucinating this whole thing?"

"Sort of. It's more like a kaleidoscope that becomes something else with each way you turn your attention. It's how you've always made up the world in which you live."

"No, no. I meant you and the wish and this whole surreal fantasy planet."

The Sun's face transforms into someone else. Someone familiar. I almost recognize that face. Who is it? Ohhh! It's my mommy, the way she looked at me when I was little and getting those stitches in my knee. The voice is hers too. *"Here's what's real as anything gets: you've got to live with what you do. But you can change what you're doing at any time. That's exactly how a wish comes true."*

I say, "Mom?"

"No more or less than Kottie," the Sun replies, its face changing again, nose growing large and hooked with bright piercing eyes. "Now make your fuckin' wish. I don't have all night."

"Wait!" I protest, "let me see if I've got this straight. The wanna-be diamond-skin bad-ass woman made a poor wish?"

"Right."

"And the horney guy too?"

"Yes, sir. You are correct."

"And you've granted wishes to a lot of other people as well?"

"Countless times."

"Then what's the best wish anyone's ever made? In terms of how it turned out for the wisher?"

The Sun flares so brightly that a hot solar wind scours my face. "Good question! Perhaps you're not as hopeless a case as your life till now might seem."

"I'm glad you like my question," I say. "But what's your answer?"

"The best wish ever made was roughly one-hundred-thirty-eight million years ago on a planet similar to your present day Earth."

"Okay. And what was the wish?"

"The fellow who made the wish was a high-ranking General in the military force that had recently conquered every nation in his world. It was a triumph that left him feeling hollow and bitter. I would tell you his name, but their language was in phonemes outside the range of the human brain."

"I really don't care about his name. What did he wish?"

"Manjooshree."

"I beg your pardon?"

"That's about as close as I can come to a human pronunciation of his name."

"What did he wish?"

"He wanted to remember who he was and what he experienced at the moment of his birth."

"Yes?"

"That's it. He got his wish."

"But what happened then?"

"Oh, about sixteen million years later the planet was toasted like a marshmallow when its sun exploded."

"I mean with the General. What happened with him?"

"Him? Nothing in particular. He just wound up in a constant state of awe and delight."

"What about his military career?"

"It very quickly disappeared. I believe he took an early retirement. To those who knew him it seemed he'd gone from a heartless, vicious, greedy bastard to a saint. He won some sort of international award for doing good. In the presentation they called him *'a freelance goodwill ambassador to all living things'*. The ironic part is that he didn't even mean to be nice. Because he was in a state of bliss, he simply brought joy wherever he went."

"That happy, huh?"

"Seemed to be."

"Then that's what I wish. To see things the way I saw them when I was born."

The Sun blinks his eyes at me and there's a sudden strobe of light.

Chapter 4 **Keepers**

There's a sudden strobe of light, then a stroke of shadow. I stand in moonlight. Silhouettes of trees sway slightly at the edge of the vacant lot. The solar space debris is gone. Was that a dream or hallucination? Something feels different. Did I get my wish?

There's my house, windows all dark. In the distance I hear a dog bark. Cell phone on my belt plays a tune. Slight breeze on my face carries the cool scent of wild mint and a subtle taste of chlorine from the pool. Also, is that the smell of rain? Cell phone's tinny music again. The clothing I wear is lightly brushing my skin everywhere. Cell phone sings. I click it on and bring it to my ear. "Hello?"

It's Kottie. He doesn't bother with salutations. "Be in my office tomorrow afternoon at one. I've already booked your flight."

There's something odd about his voice. Or is it that I'm listening in a different way? He sounds so vulnerable. Almost pathetic. Sweet taste, like strawberries, hangs on my tongue.

"Hello?" He's impatient, rushing toward anger. He needs instant obedience.

I assure him, "I'm here."

"All right then. Tomorrow at one."

I say very gently, "I don't think so."

"What the fuckin' pigshit do you mean? You don't think so? You can kiss my fuckin' ass! Be here!"

Like confiding a secret to a child, I whisper to him, "Sorry. We'll discuss it another time." I hang up and turn off the phone's ringer.

Kottie's afraid he won't be obeyed. How could I have not noticed before? Oh, yeah. I was too busy trying to obey. Far away, I hear cars humming by on a highway. I feel the weight of my body on the bottoms of my feet. Feet inside of socks, inside of shoes. The sky overhead is black with gray clouds cruising in. The horizon passes through a gradient of transparent blues. A crooked sliver of lightning breaks apart over my head.

All this that appears to be outside of me, I experience within. Even Kottie. The inside reflects the out and the out, the in. Mirrors reflecting each in the other. Where the reflections meet, that's me. I laugh out loud. Ho! I've just caught on to the cosmic joke that is myself. This *is* how it was when I left the eternal womb. The whole thing sorts itself out: I belong to the Universe to the same degree that the Universe belongs to me.

The breeze accelerates a little and rain starts to fall. I return to the house. Turn on the hall light as I walk up the stairs. Every detail is intimately familiar but seems like I've never seen any of it fully before. I stand at our bedroom's open door. Sondra's sleeping on the bed. She's naked on her belly and has kicked off the sheets.

Lately I've been thinking she was getting fat. Haven't felt aroused by her for weeks. Got to admit, right now she looks pretty good. No. Not just pretty good. *My God! She's beautiful! That exquisite plane of skin from her neck to her back! Dried tears on her cheek. I did that, made her cry. The look on her face tonight was heartbroken love! What was I thinking? I was like an enraged porcupine on the attack, slapping sharp quills of words into the hearts of those I care about most. How I wish I could take it back! I want to make love with her so tenderly that she doesn't wake up. Want to take away the frown she was wearing when she laid down.*

I undress. Feel the cool air from that breeze on my naked skin. I listen to her breathing. A little gasp catches in her throat, the ghost of a sob. Almost lightly as air, I stroke the hair on the nape of her neck. Barely brushing her shoulder tickles the ends of my fingers. I lick away tracks of tears. I don't think I've loved her this much before. At least I haven't seen her this way for ever so long.

Here, where I rest my hand on the small of her back, sensation radiates out all over her body. To the bottoms of her feet. To her ears. Her uterus. Her heart. Here, this is the skin above her calf, behind the knee. Have I ever felt before how it responds, drawing my fingers up to her thighs?

She sighs and takes a deep breath that resonates with passion even while passing through the canyons of sleep.

My fingertips find the moist lips nestled beneath her pubic arch, entrance to that most precious hole that runs directly to her soul. I enter her from behind. She raises her butt a little,

188

flutters her eyelids and whispers my name. Is she awake? No. Look. Rapid eye movements. She's dreaming that we're making love while we're making love! This is too wonderful! I lose all control! An exclamation point is an erect penis poised above a waiting vagina! I plunge to the bottom of that well of sensation. I pollinate our waiting seed! Whatever will be, will be. Will be.

I lie here beside you now. If everything that's gone before could be distilled down to just one moment, it could not be more perfect than this. I hear the rain outside. I imagine clouds made of rain. Rain in the air. Rain falling on a path of earth and stone. Roots absorbing water. Wet leaves fluttering. Wind singing through the branches of trees.

And here we are, side by side while you sleep. You are alone. I am alone. But we're each the most intimate witness to the other. Words escape into the sky. Cells divide and unite and grow a human. Patterns emerge from what seemed like chaos. Old favorites and new flavors absorb one another. I cannot leave and can't remain. I'm no longer bewildered but there's no way to explain. Except that this is it! Here I am with you!

I love you precisely because you are who you are. You give me all your pain and frustration, beauty and joy. I drink up every bit. It mixes with my own grateful tears. If you never know I've loved you this way, it won't make the blessing any less. Perhaps you think I could love someone else more. No, no. It's you. It's you. It's you.

A step or two back. I want to wake her up and make love again, this time when we can look into each other's eyes. But first there's something else I need to do. I get into my pajamas, gazing at her while I pull on a sleeve. In her face I perceive the sensuality of Lilith and surrender of Eve.

I go to the kids' room and turn on the light. I sit on the foot of Tommy's bed. "Wake up! Wake up!" I cry in a comic high-pitched voice. As they look up at me with their drowsy eyes, I say, "Hey! When's the last time I told you guys a funny bedtime story?"

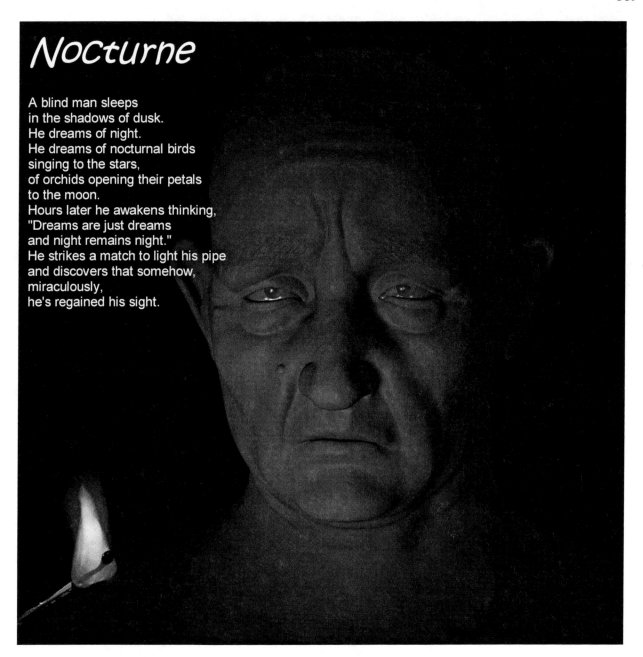

Nocturne

A blind man sleeps
in the shadows of dusk.
He dreams of night.
He dreams of nocturnal birds
singing to the stars,
of orchids opening their petals
to the moon.
Hours later he awakens thinking,
"Dreams are just dreams
and night remains night."
He strikes a match to light his pipe
and discovers that somehow,
miraculously,
he's regained his sight.

Interlude

"Let me put it this way. Artists grab at fragments of Now, but it's like trying to take home the river in a cup. Lovers enter Now doggie fashion, missionary position or upside-down. Now entertains the masses with mass in motion in extreme disguise. If all sentient beings were fish, Now would be the ocean that surrounds them as well as the ocean in each one's eyes."

Adrienne, *The Last Dragon*

Section Six

The Artists
Who Is Samuel Beast?

Information

The Artists

Sergey Zinovjev (SZ)

"I´m 39 years old. I was born in Russia, but live in Tallinn, Estonia. I´ve a family: a wife, a daughter and a cat.

Painting has always been my hobby.

After I finished school, I went to Marine College in Saint Petersburg and worked as a navigator on a ship for three years. While working there, I stopped painting, but was still thinking about my hobby and had some ideas later to realize.

I got married and started working as a car-driver. Then I had more time for my hobby and some new paintings were made. Time went on and I felt like trying something new, something that had to be connected with art - I took a rose wood and tried to make a model of it. And it worked! I started making models of rose wood till I had money to buy a computer.

Some new ideas were in my head and my computer had to render the models again and again. The 3d became my new hobby. After some web-sites had published my works, I started dreaming about 3d to become my job. One day I found an e-mail in my inbox: I was asked to make a model and the man was going to pay for this. My dream came true! These were the first money I got while making 3d. After this I started entering into the Computer Graphics industry."

SZ

SZ

SZ

SZ

SZ

SZ

IK

IK

IK

JW

SC

ZL

Igor Kudriavtsev *(IK)*

Born on June 27, 1977 in Moscow.

Graduated from the four-years course of the Moscow State Technical University and became a *bachelor of engineering science* in 2001.

In the same year he got two *Certificates* given by the Alias|Wavefront education.

From 2001 he works as a 3D artist at the Alt-Pictures TV and animated movies studio.

He is a specialist in 3D technology for such known Moscow organizations as the Argus International animated movies studio, BS-Graphics etc.

Joe Williamsen (JW)

"Let's see.... I've lived in 12 states and 5 countries and held a multitude of jobs: dishwasher, manager, construction worker and an officer in the Air Force - but I keep coming back to art. Creating what I consider "beauty" is my drug of choice. I'm currently employed as a game development artist in Salt Lake City, Utah."

Sunny Cintamani (SC) has intermittent, random ambitions, one of which is photography.

Zen Love (ZL) is a full time student of cultural linguistics, a part time flamenco guitar player and occasional artist.

Credo

Expressing insight without humor or pathos
is like having sex without foreplay or love.

Author Bio

He lives somewhere between the ghettoes and Indian reservations,
between the war on terrorism and the terrorism of war,
between gasping at the beauty and sighing in despair.

Who Is Samuel Beast?

He slides invisibly
through shifting earth planes
like a breeze
through fields of supple grain,
like an impulse
through synapses and cells
of the human brain,
like the sound of your voice
calling his name,
like the song
the holy whore moans of love,
like the heat that rises above

a flame.

Contacts

Sergey Zinovjev: sergey@samuelbeast.com

Igor Kudriavtsev: igor@samuelbeast.com

Joe Williamsen: jwilliamsen@samuelbeast.com

Sunni Cintamani: sunni@samuelbeast.com

Zen Love: zen@samuelbeast.com

Samuel Beast: beast@samuelbeast.com

The Writers' Collective: www.writerscollective.org/

Fidlar Doubleday: www.fidlardoubleday.com

Just One Now's Letter: nowsletter@samuelbeast.com

More Doggerel: www.samuelbeast.com

To Order This Book Directly From The Author:
Call 1 800 893 2783 access code 77
Or Visit www.samuelbeast.com

A Silly Little Riddle
The door opens by *pull*, not by *push*;
by *be* not by *wish*.
A little give is what's taken
if one truly wills to awaken.

For clues, subscribe to the freely given **Just One Now's Letter**, intermittent
doggerel from Beast to you. Email to newsletter@samuelbeast.com
with "*subscribe*" in the subject line. Send from the address to which
you'd like the Now's Letter to be sent.